The
WANDMAKER'S
LEGACY

MITCHELL TIERNEY

THE WANDMAKER'S LEGACY

MITCHELL TIERNEY

The Wandmaker's Legacy

Copyright © 2023
Mitchell Tierney

Published by Ouroborus Book Services
www.ouroborusbooks.com

Cover Design by Sabrina RG Raven
www.sabrinargraven.com

CHAPTER ONE
HUNTERS BLIND

Claude was standing in the middle of the forest, calling out his brother's name. Columns of trees surrounded him. He called again, but there was no answer. His heart was beating faster in his chest. He started to run through the woodland, pushing branches and fallen sticks out of his way as he called for his brother. Suddenly, he heard a whimpering, followed by a deep, heavy growl.

'Claus!' he called, running towards the growling.

Through the rotund pine trees, Claude emerged to an open clearing. He could see Claus on the ground, blood on his shirt and hands. A ginormous bear was looming over him. Its lips were peeled back showing red, bloodied gums and the hollow, hungry depths of its throat. In the moonlight, its teeth looked incredibly rigid and powerful. Its hands were outstretched, claws as black as coal. Claude picked up a fallen branch and rushed towards the bear, swinging it towards its massive paws. The bear roared with frustration, swiping aimlessly at the branch, sending strips of bark and woodchips showering through the air like falling ash from a fire.

'Get up, Claus!' Claude yelped, trying to stave off the bear.

Claus got to his feet and ran behind his brother. Blood dripped on the ground, drenching the fallen leaves. 'We have to run, Claude! You can't fight it off.'

Claude threw the branch at it like a spear and ran. The brothers bolted back through the woods, hearing the heavy breathing of the beast. No matter how fast they ran, the bear was still only a few feet behind them. They could almost feel its hot breath on the backs of their necks.

'We have to split up,' Claus demanded.

'No,' Claude replied through struggled breath. 'What if you get lost again?'

'I'll be okay, Claude. I won't go too far.'

Claus ran left and Claude ran right, each looking back over their shoulders as they went. Claude ran and leapt over a fallen tree. He saw a huddle of stones ahead. They were built up high. It looked to be a hunter's blind. He ran up them, his feet tearing through his shoes. He stopped and turned, suddenly realising the bear wasn't following him.

'Oh, no.'

He ran back down the stone structure just as he heard a howl come from behind him. Hunched over, on top of the stone hill was another bear. This one was larger and covered in thick brown fur. Its eyes glowed and its tongue lulled from its mouth from between its gnashing teeth. Suddenly, it bolted from the table of rock, down to the ground. It moved with supernatural speed, running past Claude as he closed his eyes ready for it to attack. He opened one eye and could see it heading towards the other side of the forest. A scream from a young boy, who Claude could tell was his brother, came from that direction. Without hesitation, Claude followed the bear. It was much faster than he was, but in its wake, it left massive paw prints in the forest floor. Its stride was at least four of Claude's steps. Far ahead he could hear animals barking and growling. Then, through the pine trees, he could see two bears fighting, tearing each other's fur out. On the ground by their feet was Claus. He was laying down, still as a stone. The greying bear reached for the other bear and tore its claws across its head. Streams of red splattered across the ground as the brown bear snarled and slashed at the other, repeatedly hitting it across the jaw and eyes. There was a musket shot from the boarder of the forest, then the sounds of shouting. The two bears ran in different directions.

Claude kneeled at his brother's side. His hand cradling his brothers bloodied hand.

'Claus?'

Claus's eyes shot open, wide, and pearl white. Large fangs tore from his gums, and he launched towards Claude's throat, tearing flesh from bone.

Claude shot up in bed. Sweat had drenched his sheet and matted his hair to his face. He looked around frantically. He was in his parents' house, in the lounge where he used to sleep by the windowsill. He reached for his cup of water and drunk feverishly. Suddenly, from the hallway, his mother appeared. She was wrapping her nightgown around herself.

'Claude? Were you screaming?'

'Sorry, Mum,' he said. 'I had a nightmare.'

She sat beside him on the wooden crate.

'About your brother?' she asked, moving his drenched hair from his face.

Claude nodded. She held him and rocked him gently.

'I have to head back to Mr Crenshaw this morning,' he said getting up.

He went to the kitchen and cut off a large slice of bread and spread honey over it, running the knife across it to smooth it out. The money he had brought back had paid for some provisions and medicine. He ate it and savoured every bite.

'What time is he expecting you?'

'Mid-morning,' Claude replied. He washed his hands in the bucket.

'He has been good to you,' she said. 'Good to us. It's best you don't be late.'

Claude nodded. 'I'll say goodbye to father,' he added, heading down the hall.

The door was open, and the room was cold. He couldn't hear him snoring.

'Claude,' his father said, looking over to him. He was still deathly ill. His face was waxen white, and his hair was matted with sweat, even though the room was freezing. His skin was like porcelain.

'I've got to head back to Mr Crenshaw in a moment. So, I've come to say goodbye.'

'I know you're doing… well, Claude,' he gave him a smile. 'From all you've told me… Mr Crenshaw is lucky to have you.'

Claude nodded and bowed his head. He had told them nearly everything that had happened to him since he took up the apprenticeship with Abraham Crenshaw at his wood working shop.

'I'll be back when I can,' Claude said after a moment of silence. 'With more money.'

'It's okay, Claude,' his mother said, stepping through the door behind him. 'We are fine.'

She smiled and waited as he packed his things. Much to his mother's protest, he still folded his blanket and rearranged the lounge room back to where it had been. She walked with him to the front door. Claude slipped on his shawl and pulled the hood up over his head. He rocked back and forth in his new boots and kissed his mother good-bye. He leapt from the top step onto the cobblestone street of Yorktown and ran.

He ran straight to the cemetery first. The sun was over the mountains now, peaking through white, fluffy clouds. There wasn't even a hint of rain. The smell of fresh daises and ripened tomatoes filled the air. He reached the church and saw Father Jacob ploughing a small field behind the church. He had several short tomato trees, all entwined along a wire fence.

'Well, well, well,' he said, looking up with dirt on his face. He pushed his glasses up onto the bridge of his nose. 'If it isn't Master Wells. How's the apprenticeship going?'

'Very good, Father Jacob,' Claude said, slowing down as he approached the fence. They both looked at each with a knowing glance.

'Well, off you go son, you don't want to keep Mr Crenshaw waiting.'

Claude leapt the fence instead of going through the front gate. He strolled leisurely through the meadow of overgrown grass and headstones. After a minute he was standing in front of his brother's grave.

'Claus,' he started. 'I miss you every day. I'm about to head back to Mr Crenshaw and work with him building wands and furniture. I'll come back and see you when I can.' He stood for a moment, listening intently. 'I'm still having dreams about you. They are awful and I don't know if it's you trying to tell me something, or just my imagination? I wish you were here.' He knelt and plucked some of the fresh weeds from around the grave.

He stood up and found his eyes were locked on the site of his brother's burial. It appeared to give him the energy and motivation to stay strong without him. Several large birds circled above him. He looked up and thought it was strange. They only circled when something had died. He looked back down to the grave and said his last goodbye before running out of the cemetery and down the long, winding road to Shrub Oak.

CHAPTER TWO
DUALITY

Claude found himself eager to get back to work. He missed the smell of the wood and the mysterious wands he was helping to make. The journey to Abraham's house went smoothly. A cloudy day helped him move quicker without being bogged down by the beating sun. When he got to the house, he turned the handle, but it was locked. He took a few steps back and looked up at the door. He raised his fist and knocked twice, but there was no answer.

'Mr Crenshaw! It's me, Claude!' The sun was nearly over the mountains now, casting the surrounding forests in a gloomy, dark shadow.

A soft meow came from behind the door. Claude bent down and looked under the solid, wooden door. He could see the white cat Akron standing there. He stood up and looked around the yard. *He must have headed to the shop without me this morning*, he thought. Claude left his small pack of clothes by the window and headed up the embankment of long grass until he was at the main thoroughfare. The dirt road was eerily quiet. The trees towered high above him, their branches hanging over the road like a canopy. He jogged slowly, tiring quickly as he had already walked for hours. He tried to reserve his energy by walking. He was sure he wasn't late, but if Mr Crenshaw hadn't left him a note, then the woodworking shop must busy.

Eventually, he stopped for a rest, and sat under the shade of a willow tree. The air was getting cooler as it eventually faded into the next season. He marvelled at the thick forest but noticed that he couldn't hear any birds. Spooked, he stood up, pushed his flop of blonde-brown hair back and began running again. After a few minutes, he noticed someone else ahead of him on the road. Claude slowed for a few steps as he approached the person. The figure was hunched forwards slightly, shuffling awkwardly. Claude noticed they were without shoes. Their bare feet were dirty to the point of being black with filth. When he was within a few yards, the figure looked up at him, startled.

'Sorry, Ma'am,' Claude said nervously as he glanced at her face.

The woman was young, with long, dirty blonde hair, smudged with dirt and bundled with sticks. She looked at him with a knowing smile. Claude nodded his goodbye and hurried on his way. He wanted to look back at the woman, but his instincts told him not to. As he rounded a bend in the road, he gave in to his curiosity and stole a glance over his shoulder, but she was gone. The road was empty.

The city gates of Shrub Oak were wide open. People streamed in and out, carrying wicker baskets of fruit and vegetables, they led goats on leads and nodded good day to one another. It was a vast duality from the last time he had been here, only days prior. There were no guards stationed at the gate, which

Claude found odd. High above the watchtower, he could see a man on lookout, but he neither had a sword nor a crossbow. The watchtower guard waved at him, and Claude waved back. The town seemed to be more at peace. People were mulling around, chattering, and laughing. Claude hurried through the streets and down into the dim area where Abraham had his store. As he entered the street, he could see Featherstone Antiquities had a 'closed' sign across the door. He paused briefly outside and glared in through the window. The antiques were still there but the store appeared empty, and it looked like it had been that way for a day or two. He looked down the street to *Crenshaw Cabinetry and Woodwork*. Its front door was wide open. Claude peeled himself away from the window and ran the last few yards and up the front stairs. Looking into the showroom, Claude could see the furnishings had been moved around.

'Mr Crenshaw?' he asked the empty room.

He stepped over the threshold and undid the tie around his neck that held his shawl on straight. He felt a strange twitch in his temple.

'Abraham?' he said, speaking softly.

'Back here, lad!' came his familiar, gravelly voice.

Claude bolted to the rear door and down the stairs. He could see Abraham sitting at the woodworking lathe. He was cradling his left hand with his right.

'Are you well, lad? How's your father?'

All the questions bottlenecked in Claude's mind. 'Are you hurt? Why are you holding your hand? Did you know the front door is open?' Claude said, dashing into the room and approaching him.

Abraham let his injured hand fall to his side.

'Have you taken up a role as the town constable, Claude?' he said gruffly. 'I've been turning the wheel myself since you've been gone and my hand aches.'

Claude took his shawl off and lay it over a hook. He went to the handle and started to crank it around and around. He took special interest in the wood Abraham had attached to the lathe. It was dark cedar wood. It was nearly black. Abraham picked up the file and began smoothing out the wand.

'The front door is open because I sold a cabinet, and they need it left open while they brought their cart back. I don't know if you forgot, Claude, but I am a cabinet maker also.'

Claude spun the wheel and felt his shoulder muscles pull and strain. As much as it was hard work, he had missed Abraham and the shop.

'Father is still ill,' he said meekly, as Abraham shaved chips of wood off the wand. 'The doctor gave him a little bit of medicine and it helped, but he is still in bed.'

Abraham was concentrating on the spinning piece of cedar. 'Keep faith, Claude. My father was ill for some time.'

'What happened to him?' Claude asked, noting that Abraham had never spoken of his family ever before.

Abraham looked at him through the corners of his eyes, he looked grim. Suddenly there was the sound of footsteps from the showroom.

'Mr Crenshaw!'

Abraham stood up and moved quickly to the stairs and entered the showroom. Claude stopped cranking the wheel and followed him. There was a tall man with round glasses, holding his hat in front of his stomach.

'Yes, Mr Glendale, are you all set?'

'Yes, Sir, I am. I appreciate your help. The cabinet looked gorgeous in the new bank. If I could get the second one in three weeks, that would be ideal,' Mr Glendale said, glancing briefly at Claude and nodding his head.

'Yes, that will not be a problem at all. I will send the lad when it is ready to be picked up.'

Mr Glendale nodded again, then ran his fingers through his moustache and bid his goodbye. He closed the door behind him. Claude stepped around the counter and looked at the vacant spot where the cabinet once stood. There was a perfect rectangle of dust on the ground.

'Grab the broom, lad. Get that dust out the door before another customer comes in.'

Claude watched Abraham disappear back down to the woodwork room. Claude fetched the broom from behind the reception wall and started to sweep. He wasn't sure where he would be, or what he would be doing if it wasn't for the apprenticeship. He decided to stop daydreaming and get to work.

CHAPTER THREE
HOW THINGS CHANGE

Agnes knelt down to the soft, trodden ground and plucked a gnarled piece of wood from some dead shrubbery. She added it to the bundle she was already carrying. She looked up briefly, the setting sun catching in her old eyes. A crow was high above, it circled and flew out of sight. She noted it in her mind – *a sign*. Someone is watching.

She held the lengths of wood as if it were a newborn baby, holding them to her chest, with her arm under it. Taking it inside, she plonked it down on the ground by the fire.

'Boil and bubble,' she said to the pot above the fire and laughed in only a way an elderly witch could laugh.

Lumping the flame with fresh logs, she went to her pot and lifted the ladle, taking a quick sip and running it around her mouth. She added salt, pepper and something from a bottle that wasn't labelled. Swirling the wooden handle around, she brought it up to her mouth and sipped gently. She was pleased. On the table by her workbench was an open book. The chair to the right had several pillows, all on top of the other, to give her enough height. She sat down, licked her finger, and turned the page. There came a sound of belting leather. As she turned to the window, she could see a crow had landed.

'I see,' she said, and continued reading.

The small room was slowly getting warmer, and the crow waited at the window. Eventually, it pecked twice at the glass and glanced in with a crooked, sideways look.

'I know,' she said to it, still not looking over to the bird.

She ate her stew with two-day old bread but saved a little for the crow. A large helping of butter was run across the dry bread and placed on a plate. She read the last line of the chapter she was on and turned to the window.

'I'm guessing you would like to come inside?'

The crow pecked at the glass and hopped along the sill. Agnes got to her feet and walked over to the door. As she opened it, she saw the crow leap from the window towards the door. Standing at the door was a tall man in a long black cloak. He was wearing an exceptionally large, broad-brimmed hat. His face had been recently shaven as he bore bright red rash along his jawline and neck. His long hair was tied up at the back with a velvet ribbon.

'Agnes Steelborn?'

'Yes.'

'I am Matisse. I bring you a message.'

'I figured. Come in and eat first. I assume you've come a long way.'

The man nodded and ducked his head under the door frame to step inside. He slipped his hat off and held it over his heart.

'Sit,' Agnes said, pointing to the buttered bread. She went to the pot and lapped a large serving into a bowl and placed it in front of him. He ate feverishly without apology. 'It is about the Bacre Keep, isn't it?'

'Yes, Ma'am,' he said, wiping his mouth on the sleeve of his coat. 'How did you know?'

'We've had a visitor in the last few weeks. Very powerful. Did a lot of damage.'

Matisse seemed to stare into nothingness as his mind trenched through the deep recesses of his brain.

'Bacre Keep is no more,' Matisse said. His tone was lower, and he spoke at almost a whisper.

Agnes picked up a length of wood and placed it on the fire.

'Did you hear me?' Matisse spoke, turning to her. The yellow flames dancing in the reflection of his eyes.

'I heard you.'

She sat at her lounging chair, which faced the fire and rubbed her tired and swollen feet.

'It happened so quickly… I couldn't…'

Agnes nodded, seemingly knowing what he was saying, without saying it.

'How long do we have?'

Matisse sat staring at the fire. 'They are here… now.'

Agnes nodded again. She had felt a strong magical presence but had thought it had been Ives Aries' using of the black wand. It made sense now.

'Will you fly back?'

'I cannot fly for a few days. I will never make it.'

'You will stay here. I have many spare rooms.'

'Your gracious offer is appreciated, but I cannot stay in this form for too long. I will stay in the forest. When it is time to return home, I will circle your house once more.'

'And when you return, what will you tell them?'

'I will tell them Agnes Steelborn will stop them.'

She turned her head quickly to Matisse. 'Can you not see what is before you? I am over 100 years old. I cannot pick up wood without my legs aching for days.'

'If not you, then who?' Matisse sat in quiet for some time, then shot up. 'The Three Witches of the Divine Triangle?'

'No,' Agnes simply replied. 'They have not been seen for years. They are in hiding, surely.'

Matisse rushed to Agnes, looking at her with desperate eyes. 'Then who?' He knelt down and placed his hands in hers. 'We cannot sit back and let this happen.'

'It will not be me… It will be Abraham Crenshaw.'

Matisse stood up. His hands went behind his back, and he began to pace. 'He is here?'

'Yes.'

'He is not in hiding? Like the others?'

'No. He works as a woodworker in town. He has a young apprentice.'

'An apprentice?' Matisse said, finding this notion humorous. 'How things change.'

'I will see him in the coming days,' Agnes said, her eyes now growing tired.

'I will now return to the forest to rest. Thank you, Agnes,' Matisse said, turning to her.

Her eyes were already closed.

CHAPTER FOUR
MOONSHADOW

Abraham pulled the ring of keys from his pocket as they approached the door. A cold chill swept through the hydrangea bush, giving off a lush smell. Abraham pushed the front door open and stood there for a moment, as if waiting to be confronted by the darkness that lay beyond the doormat. A flowing black shadow moved gently out of the dark. It was the familiar black cat, Maspeth. It meowed toward Abraham, rubbing its head on his legs as they made their way inside. The black cat saw Claude and meowed loudly at him and walked in the other direction, waving its tail, as if it had been inconvenienced by his return. The fire in the dining room was dim and only a few pulsating embers glowed. Abraham placed his side bag on the lower bookcase and went to the woodpile. He ploughed cut wood into the hearth and stoked it. He blew on it with care until it started to catch, illuminating the dark. The cold house was suddenly filled with light and warmth. Claude stood near the stairs as he watched Abraham tend to a pot and pour water in it, tossing in whole potatoes, tomatoes and lay an onion on the table while he looked for a cutting board.

'If you want to unpack, lad, supper won't be ready for a while.'

Claude made his way upstairs. It was familiar and unfamiliar all at once. The last time he was here seemed like an adventure, or holiday, not that he had ever really been on a holiday. Especially not one that ended in near tragedy. He placed his belongings on his bed, which he noticed had fresh sheets. He unpacked and went to the bathroom and washed his face and hands. He felt the sting of homesickness again, just like last time. It wasn't as bad this time and he knew it would pass.

After two hours, they sat and ate potato, leek and tomato soup while staring at the fire. It barely kept the cold away. The ginger cat, Oka, strolled in from the depths of the house and rubbed up against Claude's leg.

'She missed you,' Abraham said, half his face hidden by dim shadow, the other half lit by the fire.

'I'm not sure Maspeth did,' he responded.

Abraham gave a sly smile, then took it away. 'She doesn't miss anyone, lad. Don't take it personally.'

'I saw a woman walking down the main road to Shrub Oak while I was on my way to the shop.' Abraham didn't look up from his soup. 'I thought it was Agnes, the witch, at first… but as I got closer, I could see it wasn't.'

'Many hermits live in these woods, lad. Take no heed of them.'

'She had blonde hair and no shoes on. She looked… dirty.'

Abraham looked up at him with tired, heavy eyes. 'Probably lives in the woods. Now eat. We have much to do tomorrow.'

Claude took several large mouthfuls of potato, knowing food around the area was getting scarce. After he ate, he collected the bowls, and washed them in the small bucket of water. The candle near the kitchen bench was down to a stub. The wick barely staying lit in the pool of melted wax.

He turned to Abraham, to ask him what the next day would entail, but he was fast asleep on his seat. His boots were still on, and he began to snore loudly. Claude thought of waking him, taking him to his bed, but he looked comfortable. He bent down in front of him and slipped one of his boots off. Abraham stirred, mumbling something under his breath. Claude waited for him to wake, but he simply snorted loudly and continued to sleep. He clutched the other boot and slid in off.

'I'm sorry, lad,' Abraham said, the words coming out as a whisper.

'Sorry?' Claude echoed.

The fire gently lit his face. The soft glow danced around his thick eyebrows and beard, darkening his eye sockets like black diamonds.

'I'm sorry, lad,' he repeated and licked his lips.

Claude stood up. 'Sorry for what?' he asked, delicately, knowing he was talking in his sleep.

There was no response. Claude waited, looking at the old Wandmaker. The fire dimmed down to soft, beet-orange coals as it tried desperately to keep the flames. Claude fetched a large woven blanket from the couch and spread it over Abraham, tucking it up under his chin.

'Thank you, lad,' Abraham said, and continued snoring.

Claude made his way upstairs, which was noticeably colder. The chilly wind outside howled against the old glass windows. He had extinguished the kitchen candle, but not before lighting another new candle to take up to his bedroom. Just as he was about to shut the door, Akron the white cat pushed its way inside.

'Hey, get out,' Clause instructed it, holding the burning candle in one hand. 'I'm going to sleep now.'

Akron didn't give him even a glance. It jumped up on the end of his bed and curled up, making itself comfortable.

'Okay, but if you try scratch me during the night, you have to sleep somewhere else.'

Claude changed into his pyjamas and slipped into his warm sheets, blowing the candle out. The moon shone in through the window and lit a streak of moonlight across Akron. It was as if she knew the moonlight shone there. It reminded Claude of home, sleeping in the lounge room, under the windowsill. He almost felt at home now. His eyes became heavy, and he turned to his side and let sleep take him.

He woke to Akron hissing. He bolted upright in bed, rubbing his tired eyes. It was freezing cold in the room.

'What? What is it?' Akron had her paws up on the windowsill, looking out of the window. Her eyes were enormous, and her teeth were exposed.

Claude moved toward the window and Akron fluffed her tail to twice its normal size. The cat scratched at the glass hissing again. Claude took his chances and knelt over to the window to see what she was looking at, expecting it to be a night bird or rodent along the roof outcropping. Far up the hill, a quarter mile from the house, where the road cut through, were a line of lanterns, all swaying and bobbing back and forth. Claude threw back the blanket and ran downstairs.

'Abraham!' he shouted before seeing the chair empty. The blanket he had laid over him was folded up and placed on the seat. A gust of wind tore through the house, making his pyjamas sway. He turned slowly to the front door; it was wide open.

Claude ran towards the door and was about to shut it when he noticed a hulking figure in the darkness. He was frozen to the ground before he recognised the shape, and the forlorn beard. It was Abraham. He was ducking down behind a row of hedges. Claude thought about getting the candle, or a wand, but he was suddenly struck with indecision. He bolted outside, his arms around his ribcage and stomach as the icy air whipped at his skin. As he got closer, he bent down, shuffling towards him.

'Who are they?' he said gently.

Abraham turned to him. 'Lad, your skill at stealth is becoming increasingly admirable. You scared the living air out of me.'

The howl from the winds increased in volume till it

reached a cacophonous peak.

'They look like travellers heading toward the city… but no travellers I've ever seen… and why at night?'

'I need a closer look,' Abraham said.

They slowly crept along the tree line and leapt from moonshadow to moonshadow, hiding behind massive trees until they were near the road. Abraham knelt to the ground, his old knees creaking. He waved Claude closer. He pointed to a shrub that Claude thought was a little too close to the travellers. Abraham pointed to his ear, then at the travellers, indicating for him to listen. They were all outfitted in black with silver buckles and rings. Covering their heads were black hoods, some pointed upward like a spike. They shuffled slowly through the vacant, dusty road, as if they had all the time in the world. Most of them carried a macabre lantern. The handle was a demon head, with the handle ring attached through its mouth.

'…a fine place to make home,' one said.

'Yes, there is still much forest and no postings at the dock. It shall make it easier for the others.'

'It is a long way to town,' one grumbled under its hood.

'Be quiet,' said a stern voice bringing up the rear.

The one who had last spoken rode on a carriage, pulled by a pure black horse. It suddenly came to a full halt and snorted loudly, sending reams of white smog out its nostrils. The driver looked around, from dark tree to dark tree.

'We are being watched,' it said.

Abraham bent lower, keeping his head well out of sight. He could barely see Claude any longer. He had pushed himself into the shrubbery.

'It will be morning soon, we have to keep going,' said a voice from within the cabin.

The driver rehung his lantern on the hook and snapped the reigns loudly. The convoy continued their journey. Claude waited until they were completely out of sight before emerging from the under growth. He had sticks and leaves in his hair and stuck in pyjamas. He walked to Abraham, who was only a mild silhouette in the dark.

'Who are they?' he asked.

'I don't know lad, but I fear they are bringing trouble with them.'

Claude was unsure what Abraham had meant. It was possible he used sorcery to find out more information, but he wasn't going to ask him tonight. They returned to the house to find Maspeth waiting for them in the door frame. Abraham closed the door behind them, and triple locked it with chains and a heavy plank. Claude had not seen him do that before.

'Tomorrow just got a lot busier, lad. Now we must find out who they are and what they want.'

The old carpenter made his way to his bed and closed the door behind him. Claude was left on the second level landing in the dark. He looked right, through his door and outside to the pale blue, moonlit grass. It would be sunrise in several hours.

The next morning, Claude woke with the clanging of plates and cutlery. The sun had already warmed his bed and the cat, Akron, was nowhere to be seen. Claude leapt out of bed and made his way into the kitchen where Abraham had cooked two eggs each and a slither of fatty bacon.

'I let you sleep in a bit to make up for last night's disturbance. Eat up and I'll meet you outside.'

Claude nodded and took his plate to the table. Abraham slipped his boots on and went into the front garden. His three cats were out there already. They were chasing bugs and digging around the dirt. Claude ate without savouring the flavour, as he knew he was in a hurry. He dumped the dish into the cold, barely soapy water and ran upstairs to change. The cats had come inside when he passed them on the way out. Abraham quickly locked the door, checking it twice.

'We open the shop in twenty minutes, so we must get a hurry on.'

They made their way up the steep slope to the road. The first thing Claude noticed was there were no tracks from last night. The dirt was completely undisturbed. Abraham appeared to notice it also. He walked along the left-hand side all the way to the town of Shrub Oak. Once they reached the gates, Claude was surprised that they were shut. Guards were stationed at every point along the towers. Abraham walked to the side gate with Claude following at his heels. The guard recognised them and let them through. The streets inside were filled with townsfolk going about their daily business. Carts had filled the streets with fish and fresh loaves of bread. It was a mix of smells that danced around Claude's senses. As they left the thoroughfare and made their way down into the cluttered neighbourhoods of Shrub Oak, Claude could see there was a figure standing outside the shop. Before he spoke, Abraham had recognised the man.

'Lewis Galbi,' he muttered. 'Powerful wizard. He must like seeing the sun rise.'

As they approached, Abraham pulled out his keys and nodded to the wizard.

'I much prefer waiting inside,' Lewis Galbi said, with a sly smile. He had a long brown moustache and a floppy painters beret. His boots were black leather and shone as if he had polished them this morning.

'We can't talk out here,' Abraham said, his tone changing. 'Come in.'

Lewis waved both Abraham and Claude in first and followed them.

'More trouble, Abraham?' Lewis said taking off his hat and laying it on one of the cabinets. He walked as far as the middle of the room and stopped.

'Fetch the wand in the black box with the green

inlay, my lad,' Abraham asked Claude.

Claude rushed off to the rear of the store and down the stairs to the woodworking room. He pressed his back into the work bench, and it slid to the side, revealing a secret door. He yanked at the pull ring and swung the door open and rested it on the bench. Grabbing a lantern and lighting it, he made his way down into the hidden room where Abraham carved wands and imbued them with magic. It was the first time he had been down here for nearly a week. On the bench were several boxes. Two of them were black and one was red. He opened both black boxes. They were a foot and a half long and six inches wide. One had the green inlay he was after and the other had a red inlay. He placed the lid back on and took it upstairs, careful to close the secret hatch before he made his way to the showroom.

'…by the sounds of it, they entered from the docks and walked here. They may have gone to another town, but it would take them days. I need to find them and figure out what they want.'

'Abraham,' Lewis said, slightly shaking his head. 'You can't let the slightest inkling of sorcery undo you. You're jumping at shadows.'

Abraham took the wand box from Claude and thanked him for fetching it.

'You weren't here to see Ives Aries. If it is connected to him… I have every right to be worried.'

'Okay, Abraham,' Lewis took out a bundle of rolled bank notes and handed it to him. He then took the box and tucked it under his arm. 'I'm in Shrub Oak for the next few days. If anything comes of it, send the lad to get me. I'm staying at the Lamplighter Inn.'

Abraham nodded and watched him leave. Claude saddled up beside Abraham. He knew he was running several scenarios in his head.

'He doesn't seem too concerned with what we saw last night?' Said Claude. 'So, we don't need to investigate further?'

'I wouldn't say that, lad. Lewis Galbi has a knack for being more reserved when it comes to the gathering wizards, of any sort. I dare say he may have known about it already.'

Claude was staring at the door, as if it held the answer to his curiosity. 'If Lewis Galbi isn't from here, then why is he here?'

'That's a good question, Claude. One that may need answering. Now, I have to go finish some more wands before noon, can you open the shop proper and come and get me if there are any problems.'

Claude nodded and headed for the cloth to wipe down the woodwork furniture and benches.

Every hour Abraham had come up to make tea and check the store, but every time he did, Claude had everything under control. Claude had excused himself only once to use the bathroom and to finish some bread with honey for lunch but was otherwise kept busy with people coming in and browsing. By nearly two in the afternoon the showroom was cleared, and he was taking the wastepaper basket to the bins outside when he noticed a familiar gait from a person walking toward him.

'Agnes?'

The shrouded head looked up at him and she held one finger to her lips. 'Are you trying to tell the whole town I'm here, boy? For the love of everything that climbs using four legs, get inside… this is important.'

Claude found that her tone always came across as abrupt and appurtenant, rather than rude. If someone didn't know Agnes, they may think of her as offensive. The old witch hobbled up the stairs and locked the door behind her. Down in the wand working den, Abraham heard the door lock and rushed up stairs. As soon as he saw Agnes, he knew something was of grave importance.

'You look heartbroken, Agnes. If whatever you have to say can't wait until we get home, then it must be of great significance.'

'Marcus Penne is dead,' she said. The bags under her eyes looked ragged and heavy.

Abraham took a sharp intake of air and leant on the nearest table. Claude ran to get him a chair, but Abraham waved it away.

'How?'

'We suspect it was the Harrowers.'

Like a candle flickering on inside his head, Abraham shouted, 'Oh of course! That is who we saw.'

Claude was growing more and more confused by the second. Agnes looked equally confused.

'You've seen them?'

'Last night they were making their way along Pennington Road. The boy and I watched them. They were talking about making this place a fine home, and there were many of them. Upwards of 15.'

Agnes folded her wrinkled fingers in front of herself. 'The messenger, Matisse, delivered the news yesterday. He is in the forest recuperating from his journey. I thought I should let you know in case you came across him.'

Abraham nodded, but his mind was elsewhere. *If the Harrowers were proved to be the murderers of Marcus Penne, then the Wandmakers' Council will want them brought to justice.* The Wandmakers are scarce and kept hidden. It is rare skill and one often frowned upon by dark wizards.

'I suspect they will be in town for some time,' Agnes said. 'When you go looking for them, and I know you will, look for the taverns that are out of the way, something dark and hardly used. They will sleep in shifts and roam the streets at night. They are stealthy, but not impossible to find.'

'Aye,' Abraham nodded. 'Thank you for the news. I often corresponded with Marcus via letters, but in the years as the Wandmakers were hunted down, we ceased communication altogether in case they were ever intercepted. He will be sorely missed.'

'I will be out of town for several days. If you require my craft, it will have to wait,' Agnes said, heading towards the door. 'If things escalate, find Matisse and tell him to come and get me.'

Abraham, too heart swollen to speak, simply nodded. When the shop door closed, the air in the room felt stale and still.

Claude wasn't sure when to speak, or if he should speak at all.

'Who are the Harrowers?' he finally asked.

As if breaking from a spell, Abraham stood up and shook his head. 'Horrible creatures of the dark. Pirates and sorcerers. They have grown in numbers over the years, but never have set foot here, until now.'

'What do they want?'

'I don't know, lad. But if they did kill my friend Marcus the Wandmaker, then they may be after me.'

Claude looked up at his master and saw real fear in his eyes.

CHAPTER SIX
THE DAPPER HART

Abraham's mind was elsewhere for the rest of the evening. He had forgotten the potatoes in the soup and nearly burnt the bread on the open fire. He sat by the flue and stared at the flickering flames.

'I'm going back to the city tonight. I need to speak to the Harrowers and find out what they want.'

'It's too dangerous,' Claude said, emptying the pot of the remnants of the soup into a bowl. He had not seen hide nor hair of the three cats since they arrived home.

'If it looks too perilous, I will call upon Lewis Galbi. He is staying in the city. He will come to my aid.'

'I will come with you,' Claude said, already knowing the answer.

'No,' came the answer, strong and final. 'If they are at one of the taverns, then you would surely not be allowed in. I will not leave you on the streets at night by yourself. Not after all that has happened.'

Claude knew it could be perilous and agreed to stay. He watched Abraham put on his old cloak and search through boxes of wands lined against the wall. He searched through countless containers until he found the one he was looking for. It had green handle, with a dark cedar end. Wrapped around the joint of the handle was gold wire. He slipped in into his wand holder on his thigh and disguised it with his cloak. He opened the front door and a cold breeze slithered in. The night was moonless, and the surrounding lands were hidden in darkness.

'Lock the doors behind me, lad,' he said, and was swallowed by the inky shadows.

Claude did as he was told and bolted the chains around the hooks. He struggled to lift the plank of wood but managed to get it in the holding bars. He went to the fire to fill it with fresh wood, and saw that the three cats had appeared, sitting on the mat in front of the hearth, staring at him.

'He'll be back,' he told them, sitting in the spare seat, warming his hands and feet.

Abraham disliked the road at night. It was as if it had a life of its own. Shadows moved and trees swayed. Long howls from wolves echoed over the mountains and down the ravines. Soft, low winds pushed dead leaves across the road in front of him. He marched double as fast and got to the town in half the time. The gates were closed, and the guards were nowhere to be seen. He slipped through a service door and made his way around the dimly lit town. Taverns and Inns were alive with noise and musical ruckus. Drunken men made their way home, stumbling haphazardly through the streets and leaning on walls for rest. Abraham thought of what the witch had told him, *taverns that are out of the way, something dark and hardly used*. He checked the first two and could see no sign of the Harrowers. Along the western wall of the

Shrub Oak was a tavern called *The Delighted Squire*. He searched the perimeter and then went inside. The tavern was nearly empty and a small boy, barely old enough to drink, was cleaning glasses and wiping down the bench.

'Get you something old man?' he asked.

'No,' Abraham snapped, slightly perturbed about being called an old man. 'I was looking for someone.'

The boy went about his cleaning. Abraham soon found himself walking the darken corners of the town until he heard shouting and what sounded like the breaking of wood. He followed the noise to a small tavern. The hanging sign out the front read *The Dapper Hart*. The sign looked like it was well weather beaten. The paint had faded, and the windows were cracked and broken. A man pushed the front door open, holding his nose. Blood was seeping through his fingers. He shook off the daze, stepped around Abraham and went on his way. Abraham stepped inside. The entrance was filled with smoke and laughter. Men stood at the bar and guffawed and ribbed one another with their elbows. The crowd looked like the lower street dwelling denizens of Shrub Oak. Abraham thought he knew most people in the town, but he didn't recognise anyone here. The clanking of glass rattled across the bar as he made his way through the throng and motioned for the barkeep.

'Woodmaker,' the man said, giving him a recognising nod.

'I'm looking for someone,' he tried to whisper over the hoarse conversation filling the small tavern. 'A group of – '

Suddenly, his conversation was cut short by hollering coming from the far corner, near the hearth. Someone had been pushed to the ground.

'Get him up!' yelled a man missing his front teeth. His hair was pushed to one side and was greasy and black.

'Hey!' the barkeep yelped. His voice travelled far and could be heard across the room. He was well versed at yelling. 'Pick him up and dust him off and cut it out or I'll kick all of you out.'

He turned back to Abraham.

'What can I get you?'

Abraham watched the toothless man pick up the person he had just tossed to the ground. He grabbed him by both ears.

'Tell him, we'll see him tomorrow afternoon, and not a minute earlier. Understand?' He eyed him with deep moss-green eyes. When he spun around to resume his seat, Abraham noticed the same black sash attached to his cloak as he had seen the previous night.

'Never mind,' Abraham told the barkeep. 'I found who I was looking for.'

The Wandmaker turned to face the mob of heavy clad men. They were clustered around the darkest corner with only the flickering fire to keep their beady eyes revealed. The one with the missing teeth appeared to be the boss, as he ordered the others around and Abraham noticed he was holding a bag of coin on his waist belt, and the others did not. The toothless man suddenly caught Abraham's eyes and they locked together, as if about to duel. He shook his head and went back to his ale. Abraham walked over.

'I need to speak to you,' Abraham said, his voice brought down low. 'It's important.'

The men around him all laughed. They lifted their heavy tankards and walloped them across the ale-soaked tabletop.

'Get out of here, Grandpa, before you get yourself hurt,' toothless said, peering at him through his dark sockets. Thick brown eyebrows hid his pupils.

Abraham moved his cloak to one side, revealing his concealed wand. The laughter suddenly died down.

'So what?' toothless said. 'You want me to shake in my boots.'

Abraham slammed his fist down hard on the table. It shook as if experiencing an earthquake. Empty steins of ale fell over. He bent right down to toothless's face. They were merely two inches apart.

'Leave us, boys,' toothless commanded and the group moved quickly, obeying his words. 'Why don't you sit, Wandmaker.'

Abraham waited for the riff raff to eject from their seats. The last one wiped the bench seat clean of peanut shells and spilled beer. Abraham sat and the man had extended his hand out across the table to shake it.

'I am Brother Earl, owner of several transport

wagons. We don't mean no bother, so if you're here to give us an earful, don't waste your breath.'

'I'm here to ask you about Marcus Penne.'

Even in the dark, Abraham could see the flash of recognition the name brought. Brother Earl looked away instantly, then back to Abraham. One of his minions approached with two freshly poured ales and placed them in front of each person.

'Who?' Earl said, forcing his face into a confused contortion.

Abraham nearly flipped the table as he yanked out his wand and pointed the tip under Brother Earl's chin. The entire bar came to a grinding halt. The chatter died to complete silence. Abraham was on his feet. Spilled beer was pouring onto the floor. The more Earl struggled the more Abraham dug the tip of the wand into his skin.

'I got no answers for you, Wandmaker. You have to talk to the boss man, Colm Meagher.'

With a flick of his wrist, Abraham resheathed his wand and started striding for the door. Earl was rubbing his throat.

'Where is he?'

The throng of Harrowers all started to laugh hysterically. They encircled the old Wandmaker and watched with eager eyes, waiting for the word to jump in.

Brother Earl stood up. 'You see, when ashore, he likes to sleep beside the dead. It calms him,' he said followed by a maniacal laugh. 'If you want to know what we did to your friend, go to the cemetery, I'm sure Colm will be happy to answer your questions.'

Abraham flapped his long coat around as he headed for the door. He could feel his heart thumping in his chest. Just as he pushed against the door, he heard one of the Harrowers call out from the darkness.

'You know your first mistake Wandmaker... you have an apprentice. Marcus Penne was fortunate enough to know better.'

There was a cackle of high-pitched laughter, followed by the thunderous roar of Abraham firing his wand backwards and striking the man dead against his chest. Abraham marched outside into the cold night and waited for them to come out and follow him, but he suspected they had their orders.

There was only one cemetery in town, the other was in Yorktown, which was too far from the docks. Shrub Oak Cemetery was over the wall and a short walk east. There was no time to head home first and check on Claude. He would have to fend for himself if they came knocking.

CHAPTER SEVEN
THE NIGHT INSECTS

The candle's flame bobbed up and down as Claude ran his fingers through the volumes of books held on Abraham's many shelves. Most of them only appeared to have been read once and never touched again. They were covered in dust and cobwebs. Sitting on top of the second line of books was a thin tome with a red cover. Claude pinched his fingers together and managed to slip it out. He blew on the cover and still couldn't make out the title with only the candlelight. He took it over to the hearth and bent down to cast more light across it – *Timeo Solutus*. He knew it was latin, but he couldn't read latin.

A heavy thump came from the front door and Claude nearly leapt into the air from fright. He managed to drop the book on the floor and spin around to see Okra by the front door. She was staring quizzically. The darkened room became increasingly claustrophobic for Claude. He felt the air leave his lungs. Okra hissed as there came another heavy thump. Claude gingerly carried his candle over to the door. All the warmth appeared to be sucked out of the room.

'Abraham?' he stuttered. There was no answer.

He rushed to the window and looked left, toward the front door. There was no one there. Claude looked where Okra had just been, and she was gone. He heard the soft patter of her paws as she ran up the stairs and disappeared down the second level hallway. Claude placed the candle on the side table and started to unlock the door. The chains hung lose as each one was peeled off their hooks.

'Claude Wells,' said a whispered voice behind him. He spun around quickly, his eyes scanning the room for anyone. Each dark corner came alive in his mind, every shadow was ready to pounce toward him. He waited, and nothing came. The cat Maspeth sat in front of the fire, staring at him.

'I have to go outside, Maspeth. I need to see what that noise was.' The cat didn't reply.

Slowly, Claude lifted the heavy wooden plank and placed it against the wall. He turned the old metal handle and the door creaked open. The night air was cold and stale against his face. Browned leaves were knocked across the front garden and soon were lost in the raven black shadows. He stepped outside and stood on the entranceway. The night insects and birds were suddenly very quiet. Claude scanned the darkness around the house, feeling his arms burst into goosebumps.

'Abraham?' he said so softly that the wind carried it away.

The silence was broken by the crunching of leaves to his right. He turned his head quickly and caught a shadow moving among the pine trees. He stayed staring for quite some time until he decided that he would have to investigate. He reached inside for the candle and pressed it into a candle holder. He used one hand to protect the flame from the wind and slowly entered the front garden. The rocks bit hard under his feet and when he got to the grass, it felt wet and sludgy. He waved the candle in front of his face and tried to distinguish between his candle making shadows, and someone coming toward him. Overhead, an owl hooted and took to a branch. Claude looked at it. He had never seen an owl that big in all his life. He used to see them at the cemetery in Yorktown, but he hadn't seen many since his arrival at Shrub Oak.

Another snapping branch stole Claude's attention from the owl. The massive bird took to the air once again, flying across the smiling dial of the moon.

'Hello?' Claude managed to say. 'Is anyone there?'

There was no answer. He slowly took several steps forward and suddenly a shadow moved from his right, colliding with his shoulder. He dropped the candle and the flame when out. Claude was cast into pure darkness. The night was thick and all around him things moved and made noises. Something hit him on the left shoulder he spun around quickly. Fear gripped his throat and he suddenly felt as if he were trapped in a nightmare. In front of him, a flame flickered. As he stepped toward it, he could see the candle he had brought from the house was upright, and lit.

'Who did that?' he said, spinning wildly in a circle.

'Does it matter who did it? You can see now; isn't that all that matters?'

As the stranger spoke, their words slowly moved around him. He knew they were circling him. He listened intently and could only hear the one set of feet.

'Who are you?'

'I'm a friend of Abrahams. You don't need to fret.'

'If you are a friend... then state your name,' Claude ordered.

'You know, boy, I was under the impression that apprentices don't ask questions. They say, 'Yes, Sire' or 'No, Sire' and do as they are told.'

'I do as Abraham tells me. Why did you bash upon our door and hide if you are a friend?'

The voice was suddenly coming from behind him.

'I did no such thing,' said the voice as a man with straw-like hair stepped forward and exposed his full body to the dim, yellow light. He wore a dirty waistcoat and equally filthy trousers. His hands were caked in ash and his shoes needed urgent repairing. Claude thought he glimpsed the handle of a wand tucked into his belt, but it could have been a blade.

'If it wasn't you, then who was it?' Claude said, keeping his distance.

The man bowed like a clown that had finished a performance, 'Perhaps it was the wind?'

'And perhaps, it was you. Now tell me your name!' Claude said, his patience escaping him.

'Tut, tut, boy. You are getting more demanding by the minute. I guess, if Abraham Crenshaw was to return, he may want to know who came... knocking?' His eyes flashed a golden yellow. At first Claude thought it was a trick of the moonlight.

He snatched the candle from the ground and took several steps backward. Now the man was mostly in shadow, except his ratty shoes and glaring eyes.

'Tell Abraham his long-lost friend, Colm Meagher, came by to say hello,' Colm said through gritted teeth. He pulled the wand out of his waistcoat and pointed it at the boy. 'Tell him I have a job for him... several jobs. It will take some time, so he best clear his calendar. See you soon, apprentice.'

As the wand surged with energy, Abraham's three cats came bolting from the house. They tails were fluffy and their spine ridge was electrified with erect hairs. Maspeth leapt first, bringing her claws down across the assailants' hands, drawing blood. Colm yelped in pain. He had six scratches across his fingers. Akron went for his legs and tore at them as if they were a tree with a mouse at the very top. Streams of clothes and thread were torn off the man. Colm thrashed wildly, knocking the cats to the ground.

'Wild beasts!' he cried out, blood streaming from his fingers and legs.

Claude had tried to run when the attack occurred but had tripped and fallen. He was on his back watching as the cats circled the stranger.

'I was going to give you a warning shot, apprentice, but since you've taken upon yourself to attack me first, I will not show you any mercy.'

A wand inched its way out of the dark and was pressed against Colm's head.

'Tuck your wand back in your jacket,' said an unknown voice.

Colm's wicked eyes rolled around in their shallow sockets to the man who had snuck up on him. He was tall and thin and had a professionally crafted wand. The wands was painted entirely in yellow.

'I won't ask you again,' the stranger said.

Colm put his hands up, as if surrendering. He slipped his wand back into his holster and stepped slowly toward the forest thicket.

'I'll see you around, apprentice,' Colm said, fading into the darkness.

The man stood dead still, watching the dark patch where Colm had disappeared. Once he knew he was gone he turned to Claude.

'My name is Matisse. I am a friend of Agnes and Abraham. I smelt the magic pouring off him from a mile away. Are you okay?'

Clause nodded, still shaken by the attack. 'What were you doing out here?'

'I needed to recuperate. I had a long flight and don't have much energy to spare. You are lucky I had already rested a few days, or I may not have been able to come to your aide.'

'I am greatly appreciative. If you would like to rest inside, Abraham should be back shortly.'

'Thank you, but I cannot. I must rest outside. There is much I must catch and eat before I am fully recovered. If he returns, which I am sure he won't, please call my name.' Matisse bowed his head and turned on his heels, walking into the direction of the road.

After a few minutes Claude saw an owl emerge from the deep woods and fly up, across the moon. He went back inside and looked for the cats. He wanted to check them for injuries. They made themselves known to him, but they still looked frazzled. The fire had nearly died and there was nothing left but small, smouldering embers. Claude lifted a plank of wood to place in the fire and noticed his hands were still shaking. He slipped it into the hearth and sat down on Abraham's chair. He didn't mean to sit there. It was the one closest to the fire and as soon as he sat, he fell into a deep sleep.

There came a rattling at the door and suddenly Claude was awake. He leapt to his feet and snatched a length of wood from the fire, holding it out in front of him. The end still burning red. Standing at the open doorway was Abraham.

'You look like you've seen a ghost, lad,' Abraham said, marching across the room and taking the burning stake from him.

Claude, still dazed from sleep, recounted his story of the evening. When he mentioned the name Matisse, he saw Abraham's eyebrows raise.

'An old friend from long ago. I am glad he was here to help you. Now, as for Colm Meagher... I am very surprised he was able to find me this quickly. I am equally perturbed that he was here and attacked you. This will not stand.'

Abraham was pacing up and down. Outside, the sun was starting to come up over the mountains.

'He said he had several jobs for you and that he was an old friend,' Claude suddenly remembered.

'He is no friend. And it will be a cold day in hell that I do a job for the Harrowers.'

They decided to eat a quick breakfast and head to the store where they would take turns sleeping in the woodworking area. Abraham would sleep first, as he had been up all night, followed by Claude who had only a few hours. They decided to leave the shop open longer as they waited for nightfall when they could visit the cemetery and confront Colm Meagher.

equally perturbed the ... and attacked you.
This will not stand.
Abraham was ... -down. Outside, the
sun was starting to come up over the mountains.
He said he had several jobs for you and that he was

CHAPTER 8
BAD BLOOD

The night had grown cold, and the wind lashed against the windows. Abraham appeared from the wandmaking room and slammed the trapdoor down, locking it with a bolt. He slid the key into his coat pocket. Claude wanted to ask why he was locking it but thought about the presence of the Harrowers. If they could find Abraham's house, and knew that he was the Wandmaker, they would be able to find the wands.

Claude stood near the front door, waiting. He had his cloak on and his hood over his head. He was watching rats across the street clambering up the drainpipe that ran up to the antique shop.

'Do you think they'll come back?' Claude asked.

'Who?' Abraham questioned, checking the back door, and extinguishing the candles.

'The Featherstones.'

Abraham stepped beside Claude. 'I don't think so, lad. With everything that happened, I highly doubt it.'

He handed Claude a thin box in the dark. Claude took it before he could ask what it was. He opened the lid. A grey handled wand sat on a piece of dark blue satin.

'A wand?'

'I know you can use one, Claude. I knew it the

moment we met.' Claude placed the box on the front shop step held it with both hands, careful not to make it visible to anyone. 'It's yours. I've been working on it since we encountered Mage Oghast. It's only right that if I introduced you to this world, so I keep you protected. I have a responsibility to your parents to keep you safe. Now, tuck it into your cloak or belt. We best get going.'

Claude wanted to reach out and hug him but refrained. They took to the streets quickly, moving without making a noise. The wind made the old buildings creak and moan. Heavy grey clouds partially covered the moon. Abraham knew the way, as if he had been to the Shrub Oak Cemetery a thousand times. The only graveyard Claude had been to, was the one in Yorktown, where his brother was buried.

'Colm Meagher is said to sleep in the cemetery, for reasons I have yet to find out,' Abraham said, as they strolled under the partial moon.

Claude looked at him with a sideways glance. 'His men stay in town... that's what Agnes had said,' Claude struggled to keep up with the Wandmaker. Abraham was walking with urgency and kept his eyes on the path ahead.

'That's right, lad. I would say he is after fresh bodies. That would be my guess.'

Suddenly they turned a corner and marched down a long alleyway between two buildings.

'Bodies?' Claude said, hearing his own voice echo around him.

As they came to the end of the alley, they came face to face with the Shrub Oak Cathedral. Abraham noticeably didn't heed it any attention, but instead avoided it and stuck to the perimeter. Claude noticed his gaze was locked on it. Bad memories came back. They felt a little too fresh. He felt as scared as the night he had to fight for his life, and the lives of his friends.

'I fear he may be something more than just human, lad. Now hurry.' Abraham entered the eastern part of town. Claude hadn't really explored much of the town since he gained employment with Abraham. The buildings were unfamiliar. They were all old, with peeling paint and deteriorating wood and brick. The cobblestone streets were cleaner on this side of the city and the signs for the taverns and Inns were much newer and kept freshly painted.

They strolled to the edge of the city and soon Claude could feel the houses and buildings peter out. A soft fog crept over the cobblestones, giving the air an eerie chill. A wolf far over the wall and across the mountain ranges howled, and other wolves answered. Abraham suddenly stopped. His cloak flapping gently against his legs. He was staring at the rusted cemetery sign. The gates were shut, and a padlock dangled by the chain wrapped around the two gates.

'Why do they need to lock the cemetery?' Claude asked.

'Keep people out,' Abraham answered matter-of-factly.

They both approached the gate and Abraham

picked up the lock in his hand and studied it. He looked through the old metal bars and saw hundreds of headstones across the cemetery field. Thin, jagged trees scattered around them, their roots lifting up the old tombstones and making them lean to one side. Swirls of cold air whistled through the bars and over the quiet graves.

'Climb over top, lad, and fetch a stone. Something big and heavy so I can break this lock.'

Claude looked at his master perplexed. He waited for him to tell him he was joking, but Abraham only stared at the lock. Claude stepped up to the bars and slide sideways through them. It was a tight squeeze, and he had to hold his breath and angle his shoulders. Once he popped out the other side, he instantly felt the atmosphere change. It was not like the streets of Shrub Oak, or the Yorktown Cemetery, it was different. He started searching around in the dark until he found a piece of broken headstone. He lifted it with two hands and hobbled over to the gate. He angled it with great difficulty through the fence and Abraham took it in one hand and smashed it against the lock. It sent out a loud bang, echoing across the town and through the resting dead. With each hit, the goosebumps on Claude's arms intensified. Until, on the fourth hit, the lock snapped and fell to the ground.

'If that didn't wake the dead, I don't know what will,' Abraham said, pushing the gate open and slipping through. He closed it behind him and wrapped the chain around it loosely. Claude picked up the broken headstone and returned it where he found it. He felt bad for whoever owned it and wanted to come back and repair it one day. Abraham started walking straight through the centre path. It was paved with rectangular bricks with grass growing through the gaps and moss covering the top. Claude walked behind him, his arms making sure it was pressed against his concealed wand the whole time.

'Where are we headed first?' Claude said, whispering. He looked from left to right and felt the sudden squeeze of terror in his chest. It was dark and gloomy. Chirping frogs stopped their songs as they walked past them.

'We will go straight through the middle, to the very end, then work our way around.'

'What do I look for? A campsite of some kind?'

'You saw him, lad. I haven't seen him in over 15 years,' Abraham said, listening to the howl of the wind passing through the tombstones. 'If you see him, or somebody else, tell me. Stay close behind me and be ready at all times.'

Claude hadn't known that Abraham hadn't seen the Harrower for over a decade. He wondered why he had come back now, and why there was bad blood between them.

Something dark flew overhead and caught Claude's attention. He looked up in time to see a darken figure leap from treetop to treetop.

'Abraham!' he shouted, as the figure leapt toward the Wandmaker.

Abraham was able to turn his body toward the oncoming assailant just as it knocked him to the ground. The figure clawed at Abraham, tearing his cloak and leaping off him. It perched awkwardly on a large gravestone and glared at them with gnashing fangs. It was not man, nor fully a beast. It was somewhere between wolf and man. Abraham struggled to his feet. He quickly checked his abdomen, but the strikes only appeared to have penetrated his heavy, leather coat.

'So, your apprentice must have told you about our little meeting?'

'What has come of you, Colm?'

The wolfman climbed down from the tombstone. His pants shredded and his waistcoat was torn. Threads hung off his body, as did his long brown fur.

'Come on now, Abraham. Of all people… you should know.'

Abraham pulled his wand from its sheath. Claude was several feet behind him. His legs were shaking with terror. When he saw Abraham's wand, he too retrieved his. Colm noticed. A glint of the moon shone indiscriminately in his eyes.

'Tell me why the Harrowers are here, Colm.'

Abraham's voice was quivering with anger.

'We came here looking for you, Wandmaker.'

'I know you killed Marcus Penne, and you will pay for his death. But why come looking for me?'

'You see, Abraham,' the beastman said, walking in a circular motion, but keeping equal distance between himself and the wands. 'After we heard about Ives Aries, we knew where you had scuttled off to. You couldn't hide forever.' Colm paused in shadow under a giant willow tree. 'We have something we need you to do, Abraham. You see, your pal, Marcus Penne refused to transcribe a text for us. He fought tooth and bone to get away, but alas, he is now six feet under, being eaten by worms!'

Colm leapt through the air. His talons spread wide, ready to strike. Abraham swung his wand upward, releasing a blast of red energy. It flared like a bursting star, spreading fire and red clouds outward like an opening umbrella. Colm was hit in the chest and did a double somersault back, landing amongst a hedgerow.

'Get back, lad. I've lost sight of him,' Abraham demanded.

Claude stood holding his wand out in front of him. He spun it from side to side, trying to get a lock on where the part wolf man had gone. Every noise made him gasp in horror. Claude turned, his back to Abraham and saw Colm limping in the dark.

'There!' he screamed, instinct took over and he started to run toward him.

Abraham whipped around, the end of his wand smoking from the high level of magical discharge.

'Lad, no!' he yelled as he ran after him.

Colm hobbled toward the front gate and saw it was shut. He turned around, flicking his head from side to side, eager to find a way out.

Abraham and Claude had caught up to him at the cemetery gates. Colm had his arms outward, griping the fence.

'You won't get away with this, Colm. Surrender now.'

'Oh, Abraham,' Colm said. He slowly transformed back to his human form. There is no use in me running or hiding. I owe too much to them.'

'It can be figured out. You can't kill Wandmakers. The Harrowers will kill you once you have finalised your mission. Don't trust them, Colm.'

'You don't know how much I'm in for, Abraham,' Colm said, his voice staggering. 'I can't just stop. These people… they don't let you leave. I must finish this.'

'Finish what, Colm? Talk to me.'

Colm turned and leapt upward, reaching for the top of the gate. Abraham and Claude rushed forward to stop him from escaping, but Colm was too fast and scampered to the top and leapt over.

'Don't follow me, Wandmaker. I don't want to have to kill you too,' he turned away from the gate and ran into the darkness.

CHAPTER 9
LAMPLIGHTER INN

Abraham had thrown the chain to the ground and swung the gate open.

'Come on, lad. We must catch him before he gets to the others.'

Claude thought *but he said not to follow him*. He didn't make his thought known, but instead followed Abraham into the dark. They ran in pure darkness, with only a quarter moon to show the path. They reached the oil lanterns near the front gate of the town. Abraham bent down and checked the tracks on the ground. Claude was too busy trying to catch his breath.

'This way,' Abraham said, leading the way out the gate.

They followed the tracks for an hour until they eventually walked past Abraham's home. Claude could see the chimney stack from the road. It poked through the trees, leaning to one side. Once they reached the crossroads, they went right. Claude knew the intersection all too well. If they had gone left, they would have ended up at Claude's home, Yorktown. He tried not to let the memory of his parents enter his mind. He needed to focus. He knew exactly where they were going, Kincaid's Bay.

Claude and his brother Claus had done daily trips

to Kincaid's Bay to pick up fish for the local market. They were paid a penny each if they could get it back in under an hour. Claude hadn't been this way for years, way before the death of his brother. His feet were starting to tire, and he hadn't caught his breath since they left Shrub Oak. It felt like they had been walking all night when finally, the lantern light of Kincaid Bay came into sight.

There was a small dip in the road where Abraham stopped suddenly. He knelt and ran his hand through the dirt.

'He started to run here, lad.'

'We may have spooked him. Maybe we caught up to him?'

'Or he saw someone he knew,' he stood up. 'Keep your wits about you, boy. If he's cornered, he may attack again. We can't go home now and prepare. I know you're tired, as I am also, but we can't let him escape.'

They rushed down into the small cluster of fishing houses. The smell of sea was strong. The salty vapours from the crashing waves filled Claude's nostrils. Through the main street, they could see the docks. Long, running piers going out into the ocean where boats were tied to thick wooden moorings. Far on the horizon, the sun was starting to rise.

As they strolled through the stores that were beginning to open, they noticed many of the fisherman were making their way down to the boats to start their day.

'The tracks lead here, but there is no chance of following them now.'

'Where could he have gone to?' Claude said, looking at all the thin alleyways.

Suddenly, from the docks came a loud scream, followed by the sound of heavy footfalls.

'Quick, lad!'

Abraham took off running with Claude trailing behind at his heels. Claude was surprised at the old Wandmaker's constitution. He never let up along the path to Kincaid's Bay, not even to rest. As they came into full view of the bay, they could see several fishermen standing around a man lying on the ground. Abraham approached him cautiously. Claude elbowed his way past the barrage of onlookers to see the man had been stabbed. He still had the knife handle protruding from his stomach. Abraham was knelt beside him, lifting his head. He pulled a piece of wood polishing cloth from his coat and wrapped it around the wound, leaving the knife in.

'Get a cart, quickly!' he ordered one of the fishermen. 'He has to get to a doctor in Yorktown. Do not pull the knife out, it could kill him.'

Claude saw the blood soak into his clothes and felt queasy. He looked away and noticed the very last pier was partially full of boats. He saw a silhouette of a man going from boat to boat until he reached the last one and leapt onto it.

'Abraham!' Claude shouted. 'He's got onto a boat.'

Abraham left the man in the care of the locals while

he took off running down the long pier. They could see Colm tearing at the ropes and letting the sails out. The morning breeze filled them quickly and ripped the boat away from the dock. Abraham and Claude got to the edge a few seconds too late. They stood with the tips of their boots hanging off the pier and watched the boat sail out into the ocean. Colm Meagher stood on the stern, watching them.

'If we hadn't stopped…' Claude noted.

'We must always stop to help others… even if it means our suspect gets away.'

'Where is he going?'

'There's too many inlets and caves around here to know, lad. But I know someone who might be able to help us.'

'Lewis Galbi?' Claude said, looking up at his master. Abraham was still staring at the boat as it slowly faded into the fog.

'He said he was staying at the Lamplighter Inn, but first we get home. There's not use in rushing now.'

Claude agreed. They helped the injured man onto a cart and hitched a ride to the intersection. They wished them fast healing and headed back up the road to Shrub Oak. By the time they reached their house, it was daylight. They both slept and when they woke at midday, the three cats were meowing incessantly for their breakfast, as it was now nearly midday. Claude had woken first and fed the cats while Abraham made his way to the kitchen and cut them a healthy slice of bread and drizzled it with honey.

'The shop won't open today,' he stated. 'This issue with the Harrowers must come to an end first. They want me to translate a text, a request that Marcus Penne refused, and it cost him his life. As I have also refused, they will come for me. We must be ready.'

'Shouldn't we lock up the store and leave town?'

'It's best we confront this now. With Ives Aries, we had been too late, and he had risen from his place of rest. We know the Harrowers have killed a Wandmaker, and for that they cannot be left to their nefarious plans.'

Claude could hear a soft reverberation in his voice. Emotions had gotten to him.

'Will Lewis Galbi know what they want with the translated text?' Claude asked as they met in the hallway after dressing.

The stairs creaked underfoot as Abraham slipped on his tattered cloak. 'He may know. But you must leave the talking to me, at this stage, no one can be trusted.'

Claude nodded and stepped out the door. The season was turning, and the leaves were beginning to brown. The air was chilly and came from high upon the mountains. Abraham locked the door and checked it twice. He slipped his hands into his coat pockets and walked with his head down. Claude knew he was in deep thought and didn't want to disturb him until he had processed his reflections.

They were almost at the gates of Shrub Oak when Abraham first spoke again.

'Something is wrong, lad,' he said.

Claude scanned the crowd pouring out of the gates. They all looked worried. Some were carrying large bags and wheeling their carts, lock, stock, and barrel.

'Everyone's leaving,' Claude replied.

They slipped through the throng of people and Abraham picked up his speed. Instead of heading to the Lamplighter Inn, he was headed to his woodworking shop. Claude thought that his master must been on automatic, as he walked straight there without saying a word. He stopped several feet short of the front door.

'It's still there,' he said, sounding relieved.

'Did you believe it wouldn't be?' Claude said, sounding more sarcastic than he wanted to.

'I wouldn't put anything past the Harrowers, Claude. They are evil men. Bent on pure destruction. Now I have checked the shop, we can locate Lewis and get some answers.'

He turned with the flick of his cloak and started the journey toward the Lamplighter Inn. The streets were empty, and Claude felt slightly anxious. He was used to seeing market stalls and townsfolk loitering. The heavy clapping of horse hooves was another common element to town life, but now, it was deathly quiet.

The Lamplighter Inn was a three storey, grand establishment built along the main street of Shrub Oak. Abraham and Claude stood outside in the cold and looked up at the structure. It had gothic window frames, Victorian railings, and antique wainscoting.

The front door was wide open. Flanked on either side were large, black lanterns. They were lit, however, the flame was low indicating the oil reservoir was close to running out.

'Strange there is no doorman.' Claude said, remembering seeing a stocky man at the door from time to time when he travelled near the city.

'And the front door is wide open,' Abraham added. He pulled his wand from his cloak, as did Claude.

Abraham gingerly made his way up the staircase to the door and peered in. The reception desk was empty. Several of the candles and lanterns around the room had grown dim. He entered the building with Claude behind him. It felt cold in the room.

'Hello?' Claude said, glancing behind the desk.

There was no answer.

'Something is not right here, lad.'

Claude went around the desk to the ledger. An ink pot and pen were to the right. A small candle had burnt out, making the entries hard to read. He picked it up and held it to the dim light.

'Lewis Galbi,' he read. '5 nights. Paid in full. Room 34.'

Abraham listened intently, then went to the stairs and paused on the second step, trying to listen for anything coming from upstairs. Claude placed the book back where he got it and joined Abraham on the steps. They walked up to the first landing and held their wands out in front of them.

'Feels like there's no one up there,' Claude said. 'I can't hear talking or anything.'

'It's too quiet.'

With each step, Abraham stopped and listened. The landing was dark, and the only noise was the whistling wind coming through the floorboards. He stood on the last step and looked at the sign that showed the room numbers. Room 34 was the last room on the left. Claude stepped around Abraham so he could see the rest of the hallway. At the very end was a long, elongated window. The top half was stained glass, showing an idyllic mountain range and sun. The below half was a plain window. They stepped forward and noticed room 34's door was broken.

As they reached it, Claude noted the locking mechanism and handle were on the ground, busted from someone kicking the door. He knew this because the middle of the door had a perfect shoe print. All the cracks and fissures originated from that point. Abraham placed his hand backward, to keep Claude behind him. He stepped into the room. The table had been upended. There were clothes and belongings tossed about the room. The window had broken glass dangling from it. Claude noticed there was blood on some of the pieces on the floor. The four-poster bed had been torn asunder. Pieces of it lay amongst shredded bedsheets and feathers from the pillows lay about the floor.

'Abraham,' said Claude's voice in the disordered room.

Abraham was searching through the room. He had noticed drawers had been pulled out and emptied. Their contents showered over the floor with careless abandon.

'Abraham,' Claude said, his tone shaking.

Abraham turned to him. 'What is it, lad?' he yelped, somewhat annoyed.

Claude was pointing to the other side of the bed.

'Lewis!' Abraham hollered. 'Lewis, what happened?'

Abraham rushed to Lewis Galbi who was laying on the floor, blood seeping from his cut lip and a gash above his left eyebrow. Abraham fell to his knees and checked the man's pulse. He was alive, but his pulse was slowing by the second. Lewis's eyes slowly opened. They were bloodshot red.

'Abraham?' he said in a dying voice. 'They came for me... they were looking for you... but I wouldn't tell them were... you were.'

'Who? The Harrowers?'

Lewis swallowed with great difficulty as his eyes moved up to the ceiling.

'I heard them say they were going to take you to their hideout off the coast of Gloom Bay...'

'Don't talk, Lewis. We're gonna get you help.'

Suddenly, the rushing of stomping feet came thundering down the hallway. Claude spun around. His wand drawn outward. Three Harrowers in black-sash masks came pounding into the room. They moved quickly and held cudgels. One swung for

Claude, but he ducked and fired his wand, knocking the man flying through the already broken window and out onto the street. The second man leapt over the upturned seat and connected his cudgel across Claude's head. He felt his vision start to close in as he hit the floor. His head wobbled to one side, and he could see under the bed where they rushed toward Abraham. They flanked him from each side, clutching at his arms as more Harrowers came bounding into the room. Soon there were ten of them, all grasping at Abraham and pulling him down. Claude's hearing slowly had the volume turned down. With each blink he found it hard to reopen his eyes. As Abraham was dragged through the room, he was yelling something toward Claude. His face was in a panic. Claude couldn't make out what he was saying, and with his last blink, his eyes remained closed.

CHAPTER 10
THIEVES AND VAGABONDS

'Claude,' said a soft voice in his ear. 'Lad, wake up.'

Claude slowly opened his eyes. He was looking up at the bright morning sun. He sat up and his head swum.

'Don't get up too quickly. You've got a nasty bump on the head.'

Claude's hands went to the back of his head. There was dry blood. He had a throbbing headache. He glanced up at the person talking to him. He was in silhouette. The tall figure lent down, exposing his face.

'Matisse?' Claude said, his voice was groggy. 'What happened?'

Claude appeared to be outside, on the footpath. He had been propped up against the wall. There were police officers coming and going from the Lamplighter Inn.

'They're saying it was a burglary. Some of the reception cash is missing. They are saying the person who rented that room where they found you, must have tried to stop them.'

'A burglary?'

Matisse stopped talking as a police officer approached them.

'You okay, boy? Your uncle here said you had gone to visit a family friend, is that true?'

My uncle? Claude thought. It was hard to process anything at the moment.

'Yes,' Claude said, getting to his feet with the help of Matisse. 'We came by to see… him and we were attacked.'

'We?' the policy officer said. His large moustache was twitching.

'He means, *he* came by. He's had a hard hit to the head. I should take him home,' Matisse said, stammering.

The police officer looked at Matisse, then to Claude. 'Go home and put some ice on your head. It's gonna hurt for a while. We may come by in the next few days to take a statement. Your uncle gave us your address.'

Claude nodded as Matisse directed him across the road. Each hammering Clydesdale hoof on the cobblestone road sounded like a bolt of lightning.

'Where's Abraham?' Claude said, his senses slowly coming back to him.

Matisse faced him. 'He was taken by the Harrowers.'

'Where to?'

'Come, Claude. We must leave here… it's still not safe.'

Together they made their way back through to the city centre. Claude stopped to drink water and sit down as his head had started to throb again.

'Matisse, I remember Lewis Galbi saying something about Gloom Bay before he…' Claude couldn't say it. The very thought of what they may be doing to Abraham upset him too much.

'Gloom Bay?' Matisse said, as if he should know the place. He chewed the words over in his mind.

Matisse helped him up again and quickly helped him through the crowded alleyways.

Once they reached the city gates, Claude put his hood up to protect his face from the sun. His eyes were hurting, so he kept his gaze down towards the ground. Matisse would often stop briefly on the way back to Abraham's house to catch his breath. Claude thought he became breathless easily and wondered why he required so much recuperation.

As they neared the exit to Abraham's house, Matisse stopped suddenly.

'Gloom Bay,' he said, somewhat perplexed. 'Yes, of course. It's been called so many things over the years. Do you know of Gloom Bay, Claude? Or its other names, Skull Inlet, or Thieves Haven?'

Claude shook his head. 'I've not heard of it before.'

'From memory, it's a small peninsula not too far off the coast. Many years ago, it was used by pirates to ambush incoming ships. The great battles have been written in the history books. Some tell the tales of sunken ships and treasure. It is not a good place, Claude. It is the home of thieves and vagabonds.'

'Why would they take him there?' Claude asked.

'The Harrowers are more than likely based there. I'm sure most of them are here and more are on their way.'

Claude was trying to retain as much information as possible. He was still sore from the attack and wanted rest badly, but knew time was of the essence.

'I have to go and find him.'

Matisse looked at him worried. 'I'm sorry, Claude. I cannot come with you. Not in my state.'

Claude didn't want to pry any further. He had more pressing matters to be concerned about.

'I will go alone. Under the cover of darkness. I will find him.'

Matisse rested his hand on Claude's shoulder and gave him a faint smile. 'God speed, young Claude.'

He turned and hovelled back into the thicket of the forest. Claude was suddenly left alone, on the road. It was cold and he felt like the only soul within miles. He turned and rushed back to Abraham's house. He stopped feet from the door and saw the front door was wide open. His blood ran cold.

Slowly, he crept up to the door and peered in. He couldn't hear anything. Claude took a singular step inside and saw Maspeth at the foot of the stairs, looking up. Claude must have startled her, as she turned and hissed at him. The hair on the ridge of her back was on end. She bolted into the kitchen. Claude wished he could talk to them.

There came the sound of scraping from upstairs. Claude stepped into the room and closed the door. He was gentle not to make a peep. Reaching to his side, he slid out his wand. Step by step, he carefully made his way up the staircase. With each step, he was careful to adjust his weight and stay clear of the creaking boards.

As he crested the top, he saw Oka, the ginger cat. She was staring in his room. Her hackles were up, and her tail was puffed. She hissed at something in Claude's room. He bolted forward with his wand in front of him. Quickly, he kicked his door open all the way to see a shadow dart out the window. He leapt across his bed, giving the intruder a chase, but it took off quick. It tumbled over the awning and down the drainpipe like it had done it a thousand times.

Claude ran from his room, stepped over the hissing ginger cat, and rocketed down the stairs. By the time he reefed the door open and sprinted outside, the intruder was gone. He stood holding his wand, scanning the surroundings. Nothing moved and nothing made a noise. From behind, he heard the soft patter of cat's paws on the pebbled entrance. Turning around, he saw Oka, Maspeth and Akron all standing beside one another.

'It's Abraham,' he told them. 'He's been taken to Gloom Bay and I'm going to get him.'

The cats looked at one another. They seemed to understand, but it was too hard to tell. They stood in front of him, as if waiting for instructions. Oka started to clean her tail.

'I'm waiting till nightfall, then I'm going to get him.'

This made them somewhat satisfied. Claude took his boots off and noticed they were thick with dried mud. He took them to the rear door of the house and sat on the stone steps. He felt prickles in his eyes as he peeled the mud away. They were the shoes Abraham had given him.

One by one, tears streamed down his face. He felt the warm touch of a cat, as it rubbed up against him. When he was done and had wiped the boots clean, he stood them by the front door. Everywhere he went, Maspeth followed. He heated water and took it to the bathroom and filled the metal tub and washed himself clean. He felt the bump on his head and winced. There were a few hours before he wanted to leave, so after he was clean, he lay on his bed. He stared up at the ceiling and thought of what he was going to do. It was hard to plan when he didn't know what he was going into. How was he going to get to Gloom Bay? Where would the Harrowers be hiding? Is it too late?

The thoughts rocked him about and his throbbing head kept him from lying on his back. Soon enough, utter exhaustion took the better of him and he fell into a deep sleep.

When he woke, there were two giant yellow eyes staring at him. He nearly leapt out of his skin before he noticed it was Maspeth sitting on his chest staring at him. He picked her up and moved her to the side and sat up. It was dark outside. It was time to go.

He slipped on his breeches and thick woollen socks. He put on his waistcoat and clipped his wand holster to his right thigh. His poncho with the hood was placed overtop and he instantly felt it hold in the heat. Sitting on the last step near the door, he tied up his boots. The cats appeared from the dark recess of the house and watched him, curiously.

'He's coming back, I promise,' he told them and stood up. He picked up his wand and studied it from tip to handle. It was magnificent. It felt strangely part of him. He placed it in its leather holder. Then, he went to the kitchen and found a small knife. He placed it safely in his waistcoat and headed for the door.

The wind was brutally cold outside. Clause brought his hood up, over his head and held it tight to his body. He walked down the long path to the road and hurried up the escarpment. The road was empty.

A howling wind tore through the tree canopy overhead, as if heeding him warning. He started his trek by going left, toward Kincaid Bay. The night was darker when you walked alone, Claude thought. He could hear every one of his steps echoing like rolling thunder. Bats all around him screeched and justled for position on branches. Occasionally they would swoop in front of him, checking if he was a stray mouse or rabbit. After an hour and a half, he could finally smell the salty sea. Only a few minutes after that, he could hear the crashing waves on the boats and foreshore.

As he breeched the sandy dunes, he saw the lanterns prickling a small village. Everything seemed quiet and calm. He felt his pocket for the few coins he had collected as tips from buyers at Abraham's store and headed into the town. Fishermen always got up early. They believed fish slept and had breakfast. Claude felt eyes on him straight away as he walked through the dimly lit centre. Fishermen were carrying empty crates down to their boats, as well as fishing reels and stinking old hooks and bait.

'Sir,' Claude said to an elderly man eager to get past him on the cobblestones.

'I ain't got nothing to give you kid, go ask someone else.'

Claude was struck by the rudeness, but let the grumpy man continue his way. He followed the men and women down to the dock and watched as they readied their boats. Claude decided to go far to the end and ask each one if they would take him to Gloom Bay. The first boat looked to be run by a husband-and-wife with two small children. The kids were hauling ropes and busing themselves with work.

'Excuse me,' Claude said politely.

Everyone suddenly stopped what they were doing, as if frozen in time, and stared at him.

'I require passage to Gloom Bay. And I was wondering if…'

'Why would you want to go to Gloom Bay?' asked the wife.

'It's my… uncle,' he lied. 'He's gone there, and I need to see him.'

The father slammed down the fishing gear he had been carrying and took several sharp steps toward Claude.

'Then your uncle must be as crooked as these hooks!' he pronounced. 'No one goes there for good intentions. Criminals!'

Claude bowed his thank you and continued to the next boat.

'Sir,' Claude started.

'I heard what you said, young chap,' the man said, continuing to loop in his large rope. He placed it on the side of the boat. 'I may look as old as this here pier, but my hearing is still good.'

'Could you take me to Gloom Bay?'

The fisherman turned and stared at him. His beard was snow white, as was his moustache. He wore an old captain's hat that was haggard and frayed around the edges. He wore dirty clothes, with holes in the armpits. Out of all the boats in the dock, his looked the newest.

'I can always use a shipmate. I'll tell you what, I'll take you to Gloom Bay, but I won't be pulling into the dock there, no young chap. You see, they'll have my boat and all my possessions in a quick instant. If you help me do my lines and secure the crab traps, I'll take you close enough to swim to shore. Is that a deal?'

Claude couldn't swim. 'Okay, Sir. My name is Claude.'

The boat captain held his hand out for Claude to shake it. His skin felt full of callouses. It was hard like stone, and his fingers were gnarled and constantly bent inward.

'My name is Seymour Lugworm. But people know me here as Lug. If you tell 'em Lug got you there, they'll know who you're talking about.'

Claude climbed aboard and was put to work straight away. He straightened the fairlead and pulled the jib sheet closer. His arms were already starting to become tired. Soon, they were on the open water, ahead of all the other boats in dock.

'You know why I do so well, young chap?' Lug asked, yelling against the plumes of sea water. 'I go to places no one else goes. You're lucky you got me when you did. No other boat goes that close to Gloom Bay except me!'

Claude wiped the sea water from his face. The salt was stinging his eyes. 'Why is that?'

'My boat is quicker. Faster when two people are on it, but my other sea-hand quit last week. He kept vomiting from the rocking waves,' Lug laughed out loud. His large mouth showed missing teeth and a purplish tongue. Claude thought it was quite a sight. 'Gloom Bay is full of people that abide by no laws. They're merchants of black-market trade. They aren't allowed in Kincaid Bay, you see. So, you say your uncle is there?'

'Yes, I hope so,' Claude replied.

Lug nodded feverishly. He didn't ask any more questions while he concentrated on sailing out of the bay and into open water.

CHAPTER 11
THE TOME OF MANY WHISPERS

Claude had tossed the last crab trap overboard and watched the deep blue ocean swallow it. The rope beside him was yanked into the water so quickly it became a blur. He held the floating device in his right hand and waited to make sure the line hadn't tangled. When there was a metre left, he threw it into the air. It landed on the ocean surface with a heavy slap.

'Well done, chap. You'll make a good deckhand one day if you choose to do so,' Lug said, spinning the wheel far to the right.

Claude sat down and watched the dots of islands around him grow bigger. They passed many of them. They were quiet and spooky to look at it. Most of them had palm trees that swayed in the wind eerily. He knew why the vagabonds chose this area, it was isolated and a complete maze of islands and inlets. Between two large rock canyons rising out of the water, Claude could see another boat. He looked toward Lug, who had already seen it.

'Don't worry yourself, young Claude. Ships pass through here during the day, as well as night. If they leave us alone, we will leave them alone.'

Claude turned back to the boat in the distance, but it was gone. He sat in silence and wondered how long it would take to get to Gloom Bay. As time went on, he started to figure out why people stayed clear of this area. A gentle fog started appearing on the water's surface. As they approached it, it grew thicker and thicker. The towering walls of rock around them seemed to become hands of underwater giants, reaching up to nab them from the ocean's surface. Claude felt the boat slow down. The sail behind him was yanked and the wind went out of it. They were drifting now through terrain they could not see.

'It's coming up here, chap,' Lug said. His voice was nearly a whisper. 'I'll get you close to the isle in-ways, and you can jump across to a landing and walk your way over. If you fall in the drink, you're on your own.'

Claude stood up and gathered his wits. He stretched his fingers out wide, then readied them. Lug yanked at the steering handle and set the ship careering sideways. Claude saw the rocky landing coming closer and closer. For a moment he thought they were going to collide with it.

'Now, young chap!'

Claude leapt and splayed his arms outwards, his tunic flying out behind him like a cape. He landed on the hard rock and began to slide down. Lug yanked the handle the other way and pulled at the rope that controlled the sail. The ship nearly went over, but Lug managed to pull it back from near collision. Claude reached for a stray tree root growing out of the rock escarpment, but as soon as you gripped it, it broke off in his hands. He fell a further three feet and tried latching onto anything he could.

Finally, he gained purchase on a sharp bit of overhanging rock. His feet were dangling over the edge. Pieces of stone and dirt crumbled down on his head and spun carelessly until it hit the water. Claude reached up with all his strength and clutched a more durable tree root. He tested it by pulling at it. When he knew it was strong enough, he pulled himself up. With one hand after the other, he reached the top and lay on his back.

Far in the distance he could hear shouting and the clanging of blades. He sat up and looked toward the ruckus. Two men were fighting with swords outside a shanty building. Claude rushed to his feet, turning quickly to see if Lug was still in the vicinity, but all he could see was the tip of the ship being swallowed by fog.

'Critten!' one yelled as he thrust his sword into the defender's stomach.

There was a horrible squelching sound as the opponent's eyes popped open in genuine surprise. His fingers spread wide, and the sword dropped to the ground. The man held his stomach as he fell to the ground. His head slowly turned toward Claude and he smiled and rolled onto the ground. Many men in hooded garments flocked to the scene. They surrounded the men quickly and with a flurry of moment, they carried the men away.

Claude wasn't sure what to make of the whole situation. He wanted to flee, but now he was trapped. There was silence for several seconds before the rowdy noise began up again. Walking toward the hut, and feeling wet from being on the boat, he stopped short of the where the battle took place. There was blood on the ground. The tavern had a sign, with words burnt into it by a branding iron – *The Foggy Alehouse*.

Outside of the tavern were empty barrels with rusted iron bands. A mangy dog scratched its ear and looked at Claude indifferently. An elderly patron had passed out near a wagon and fallen asleep. Claude didn't want to enter the establishment and ask for directions, so he sat beside the barrels and watched the fog roll in over the sporadic, rocky canyons. He thought about the prospect of Abraham being dead and it brought tears to his eyes. He wondered how he was going to free him from the hands of the Harrowers, and he suddenly missed his mother and father. He wiped a tear away and got comfortable as darkness descended upon Gloom Bay.

He woke with the sound of men shuffling past him. One accidently kicked his boot and made no attempt to apologise.

'Stray's,' the patron grumbled while pulling his hood up over his head. Suddenly a flash of memory sparked across his vision. It was a face he had only seen for a split second, but it was memorable. It was the face of the person who knocked him unconscious in Lewis Galbi's room. The fleshy bump still raised on his head started to throb, indicating that Claude was not imagining things. When they rushed around the corner, Claude stood up and began to follow them.

The hill slanted upwards and was floored by round, grey stones. Moss covered the ground, and the cloudy water vapours made it slippery. Flanking each side of the path were mangroves. Their salty smell gave them an aroma of fish and mud. Slowly, the path twisted up and around boulders and exposed roots. Claude didn't want to catch their attention, so every few feet he moved, he hid behind a tree or crouched down behind a boulder. He looked for other ways around, to try and catch up to them, but on either side the mangroves were so thick, it made it impossible to pass. He peered out from a large shrubbed bush and saw the men's feet disappear around a sharp corner. He rushed up the path, stealing a look behind him. The path was getting steeper and more slippery. Ahead, he could see the path had several bends and turns, but there was no sight of the two patrons. He stopped briefly and looked left and right, trying to locate them through the thick undergrowth. *Perhaps they had begun to run?* he thought. Quickly, he moved up the hill and through the winding path. Before too long he reached a straight, narrow piece of flat path. He could see it was 30 feet in front of him until it opened to a small town.

'Where did they go?' he said quietly to himself.

'Not so sneaky now, are you kid?' said a voice from behind him.

Claude spun around to see one of them men pulling off his hood. It was the man that had attacked him.

'What do you think, Jolly? Kid seems to be

following us up the mountain.'

From the thick brush emerged the second Harrower. He stood on the opposite side of Claude. He was now stuck in the middle.

'I think he knows who we are, Mathian. We saw you jump from the ship, kid,' Jolly said, now addressing Claude. 'Only one reason people come here... looking for someone.'

Claude couldn't step forward or backward. He was trapped with the mangroves on either side of him. The wind started to thrash as if a storm was about to pass over. Cold sea water whipped his face.

'I'm looking for Abraham Crenshaw,' Claude said.

Jolly looked at Mathian. The grin on his face dropped.

'And what do you want with the Wandmaker?'

'He was taken... by you, to this island. I'm here to free him,' Claude felt a swell of pride and courage as the words left his mouth.

'Is that so?'

'He's a troublesome old coot!' Mathian gnarled. 'When he's finished doing what we say... he'll be set free.'

Jolly laughed and Claude knew he wasn't telling the truth. He slid his hand into his cloak and pulled out his wand. Mathian saw it and pulled out a club that still had Claude's blood on it.

'There's no way home for you, kid.'

'After the sharks eat you, there will be nothing left,' Jolly scoffed and lunged toward Claude with a thin, rusted knife in his hand.

Claude dodged to the side, feeling the knife whistle passed him. It cut through his cape and tore a hole in it. From behind, Mathian swung his arm toward Claude's neck, trying to catch him in a chokehold, but Claude was too quick and ducked out of harm's way. The two Harrowers became increasing frustrated as they launched themselves toward the small boy. Claude rolled across the ground and brought his wand up, letting a stream of orange coloured energy pulsate from the tip. It connected Jolly in the chest and sent him backward into the mangroves. Mathian rushed forward and was able to get a strike on Claude. His wand flew from his hand and rattled across the stones until it landed in the mud. Mathian had a grimace upon his face. He seethed through clenched teeth.

'Your friend Abraham only has to do as we say, then he'll be dropped back into the ocean. You don't need to worry about anything, kid.'

'What are you having him do?' Claude said through narrowed eyes.

They circled each other like caged animals. Claude was trying to get close enough to his wand to clutch it from the mud.

'All we ask of him is to translate an old book for us… it isn't hard.'

'Why kidnap him then?'

Mathian swiped a hand forward, trying to catch Claude off guard.

'*Frenguard – The Tome of Many Whispers* can only be translated by a Wandmaker. And your friend, Abraham has thus far, refused.'

Claude had never heard of the book. He also had never heard Abraham mention it.

'If my master refused, then it must be a book of evil. He has every right to refuse.'

Mathian laughed at Claude's suddenly outburst.

'The Wandmaker Marcus Penne also refused… and now he is dead. His whole shire of Bacre Keep was burnt to the ground, with him in it. You don't want that to happen to your master, do you?'

Claude leaped toward his wand and snatched it from the mud. He pointed it toward the Harrower, striking it from left to right. Long strands of red lava-like energy carved through the air, sending Mathian toppling backward. He gained his footing quickly and speared his body into Claude. This time Claude held onto his wand tight. He fell back and clipped his shoulder on an exposed boulder. He felt it tear at his skin and clothes. Wetness followed through his body. He knew he was bleeding, but the Harrower was now on top of him.

'Jolly!' he called out. 'Bring me the knife!'

Jolly rushed out of the mangroves and placed the blade in Mathian's hand. He held it high over his head.

'You've done well kid coming this far, but this is where your journey ends.'

He brought the knife down, trying desperately to

lunge it into Claude's eye, but Claude was quicker.

He had never heard the word that escaped his lips before. It wasn't in his common language, and he didn't know what it meant, but the wand reacted as if a fireball had been cast from it. It lit the entire mangroves up in a flash of red and yellow. Claude closed his eyes and felt the heat radiate all around him, but it wasn't burning his body. After a few seconds he reopened his eyes and Mathian was burnt nearly to ash. He pushed him off and scrambled to his feet. Claude was quickly wiping the ash off him when he noticed Jolly had been further away. He had still copped most of the flames, but he was still alive, barely. He was trying to crawl up the hill. His coat still on fire and his feet smouldering. Claude rushed over to him.

'Where are you keeping Abraham?'

Jolly looked at the young Wandmaker. His eyes were bloodshot red, and his face was peeling.

'If I tell you… they'll kill me.'

He took one long intake of breath and stopped moving. Claude stood over him. He hadn't noticed he was still holding his wand. He tucked it in his coat and started to search the man for anything that may help him find his master. In his left, inside pocket he felt something heavy. He reached in and pulled out a key. He held it up to the sun, that was nearly completely blocked by grey clouds. It was silver and had an emblem on the end of it. Three rabbits chasing their tails.

CHAPTER 12
COMMON COURTESY AMONGST THIEVES

The rain came in from the west. It smelled of ocean water. Claude pulled his hood over his head and trundled through the mud. Once over the hill, he could see the ramshackle town. To the east was a cropping of rock, then it fell off into the ocean. To the west was a jungle of thick trees and shrubbery.

He halted at the stone staircase and tried to look for signs or street names, but there weren't any that could be seen from this height. He slowly stepped down. The stone steps were covered in green moss and slippery from the rain.

He knew it would only be a matter of time before someone found Mathian and they would be after him. As he approached the town, he could see multiple figures dressed in black scattered throughout the area. They had their heads down and tried not to make eye contact with anyone. When Claude stepped through the entrance, they paid him little to no attention.

The roads were uneven stone bricks with mud as grout. The horses tied to bannisters were skinny and covered in sores and fly bites. They kicked and grunted excessively. All the stores were put together from Beachwood or anything that had washed ashore or brought over from the mainland. Ropes, bleached white, held most the construction together. An old ship, that had been turned on its side was being used to sell hooks, anchors, and spears. The seller spotted Claude and waved him over.

'Hide yer face all you want, laddy. Your pa should not be lettin' you out wandering around here.'

Claude nodded his understanding and continued his way. Ahead of him were even more people. They stumbled around and pushed one another in what was a dilapidated saloon. From somewhere inside he could hear a moan, followed by a cheer. It was the most people he had seen yet, in one location. He saddled up to the other itinerants and pushed his way through the throng. There was no door on the saloon, only an archway made of dry coral and sticks. He walked through, keeping his face disguised for the time being. No one paid him a second of attention. They all looked like sea faring folk, hard weathered and sickly. He had seen them in the city pulling carts of stinking fish, a long trail of cats behind them.

'Watch out there,' one disgruntled customer griped. Claude had bumped into him as he made his way through to the bar.

The bartender was a young woman with slick black hair done in a ponytail. She was the cleanest person Claude had seen on this island yet. She wore a frilly white top with a thick leather belt. She nodded to him, then looked at him more intently.

'No children in here. Sorry, lad.'

'I'm looking for… my pa,' Claude quickly said, at half a whisper.

'I don't know anyone's name, son. Best you get out of here.'

Claude stepped back as large men pushed passed him and demanded ale from the barkeep. Claude knew it was a long shot, but he thought at least he could try. The stench of the men, the spilled ale, and the blood from fighting was starting to make him gag, so he headed for the door. Outside, the fresh sea air came as a sweet relief. He would check every house and store and shanty hut if he had to. There wasn't much here, and he would do it even if it took all night and the next day.

After two hours of searching, Claude thought perhaps, they had taken Abraham someplace else. He started to lose all hope. He stood still and breathed in the ocean air. A man leaning on a boat on harbour stilts caught his attention. He was wearing an oversized, floppy, black captain's hat and polished black shoes with large silver buckles. On his hip was a loose belt with a rapier in its sheath. He was smoking a long pipe with one hand and playing with a coin with the other. Claude tightened the cord around his neck, bringing the cape tight around his shoulders. He began his walk over to him.

'I know what you're gonna ask me, kid,' the man said, without looking up to greet Claude's face.

'I don't know how you can, but I'm after my…'

'Master. A Wandmaker, right?'

Claude took another step toward him in astonishment.

'How did you know?'

'I've watched you ask half the island for your pa. No one here's kids are looking for them, trust me,' he took a long draw of his pipe. 'I saw them takin' him through here. He's tough. They had great trouble trying to get him under control.'

'That sounds like him. Is he hurt?'

'I would say so,' the mysterious man said. 'They flogged him with leather and ended up branding him with hot iron.'

Claude gasped and felt prickly tears build in his eyes.

'Where is he? I need to find him.'

The man flipped the coin in the air and looked up to snatch it from the sky. Claude could see he had a blackened beard and tucked back ears. His moustache was curled, and he had glassy, near golden eyes.

'Heads I help you, tails you walk away.'

Claude looked at the man's hand. He wasn't sure what to do.

'I'm Claude Wells from Yorktown.'

The mysterious man eyed him under the brim of his hat.

'No one uses their real name here, Claude Wells from Yorktown.'

'Why not?' he asked, eager to see the coin.

'No one here is who they say they are. So, there is no use.'

'Then, what is your name?'

'Valiant Seawright. Captain of the Golden Serpent.'

'And that isn't your real name, then?'

Valiant nodded. He slid the coin into his pocket without revealing it.

'Follow me, Claude Wells of Yorktown.'

Valiant stomped his feet twice and took off marching through town. Claude started following him before he could even ask where he was going. Valliant's coat tails were flapping behind him, as was the smoke from his pipe. It smelt exotic. They marched through town as if they needed to escape before being seen. Valiant turned suddenly and wiggled his way beside two shanty buildings. On the other side he ducked into an abandoned house. Claude had followed him all the way until the house doorway.

'Come in, kid. Do you want them to get the bounty on my head?'

Claude apprehensively strolled in and shut the door.

'You have a bounty on your head?'

Valiant laughed loudly. His laugh was more of a cackle, like breaking firewood.

'Everyone here has a bounty. That is why we are here! Do you not have one, Claude Wells of Yorktown?'

Claude shook his head. 'No.'

'Well, you must be the only one.'

'What do you know about my master?'

Valiant pulled up an old wooden chair and sat on it, crossing his legs. He pulled his tobacco pouch from his long coat.

'He's being held captive, across the street from this very elegant abode.'

Claude nearly jumped out of his skin. He spun around and bolted to the window.

'Ah, ah,' said the pirate. 'If you go over there now, they'll kill you.'

Claude peeled a piece of rotting board from the window and peered out. The ramshackle house across the muddy way was completely boarded up. It was three levels. Every window was missing its glass. In its place were sheets of timber board.

'What do they intend to do with him? He might be dead for all we know.'

Valiant packed his pipe and then sat on a bundle of rags and dirty sheets that he had made into a cot. His boots were layered in mud and sand.

'He might be dead, however, every night I hear him howl in agony.'

Claude felt a heavy stone in his throat. He fought back tears.

'I hope he's okay.'

'Tonight, will most likely be the same. From what I hear, they want him to read something. Translate it into their language.'

'Then tonight we rescue him.'

'We?' Valiant said. 'I hope people stay out of my business, and I stay out of theirs. It's a common courtesy amongst thieves.'

'I'm not asking you to get involved in their

business,' Claude said, placing the panel back. He turned to the mysterious pirate. 'I'm asking you to help me get him out.'

Valiant rolled forward and knelt on one knee. He gathered up small pieces of wood that had peeled off the house and placed it on a metal plate. He lit it with his match.

'I come here to make money, not die trying to free someone I don't know. Plus, there are many of them, not just the two that had brought him in.'

'How many?' Claude asked.

Valiant shrugged, while reclining back onto his rags. He shrugged. 'Could be three, could be twenty.'

'I'll watch the house and see how many come and go, then we will know what we are dealing with.'

Valiant raised an eyebrow and took his hat off. His hair was midnight black and resembled straw. The sun and the sea water had turned it stiff and angled.

'There's still the matter of…'

'We will pay you. You help rescue my master and get us on your boat and back to Shrub Oak, and we will pay you well.'

Valiant rolled his eyes, pondering the offer. He brought his pipe up to his mouth and took a long drag while eyeing the boy.

'Wandmakers in general have little money. How can I be sure…'

'He owns a cabinet making business in town. He's very popular, always busy. I work there and he pays me well.'

'If this is a ruse boy, I will burn that business to the ground.'

Claude nodded. 'Deal.'

Valiant wiped his hand on his dirty trousers and held it out for Claude to take. He gripped it and shook it. The pirates hand felt grimy and sandy.

'We wait till midnight, then we go in. They would have had their fill of ale by then and ready to sleep.'

'Midnight?' Claude said, thinking how long it was away. He finally shook his head, giving in to the plan.

'You may as well get some shut eye. It might be an eventful night.'

Claude lay down on the floor in the corner with full view of the window. It smelt like fire smoke and the sea. He fell into a deep slumber while listening to the pirate snoring.

CHAPTER 13
THE DEAD OF NIGHT

Claude woke to the heavy footfalls of men outside. He shot up in bed, startling Valiant, who had grabbed his pistol. Through cracked wooden panels, Claude could see it was the dead of night. The moon was waning, high in the sky and white as an unlit candle. Claude got to his feet and knelt by the window. Four men were drunkenly returning home from the Foggy Alehouse. They staggered and fell over one another. One of them started to urinate in his trousers. Claude looked to Valiant who was warming his hands in the dying coals of the fire.

'I told you Claude Wells of Yorktown, just on time. I should change careers and be a fortune teller.'

Claude turned back to the window in time to watch the men stumble inside. He could hear the locks being drawn across the door, followed by someone else yelling.

'Sounds like they are getting in trouble,' he said, at a whisper.

Valiant nodded. 'It will be their turn to watch the prisoner in a few hours, I would imagine.'

'Why do they want Abraham to transcribe the book? Why is it so important to them?'

'Have you heard of the deathly pirate Pablo Marquise?'

Claude shook his head. He had never heard of any pirates, ever.

'No,' he answered meekly.

'They called him the Ravenous Pablo Marquis. You see, he was cursed by a witch and tied to cinder blocks and dropped into the ocean. The exact location is unknown, so he sits there, attached to chains at the bottom of the sea, being eaten by fish. It is said that due to the witch's curse, he is still alive, awaiting the day he is freed, to breathe on land once again.'

'Why did a witch do that to him?' Claude asked.

Valiant raised an eyebrow, as if it were too sacred to speak. 'He stole from her.'

Claude looked at the pirate's face. The embers from his pipe lit his face in red. Oblong shadows danced across the bridge of his nose.

'He stole the book?'

Valiant nodded.

'He wouldn't tell her where it was, so he was doomed to live the life of a crab.'

Claude didn't like the sound of that at all. It made his throat tighten.

'If translated correctly, it will show his exact location and how to free him from the witch's trap. Or so the rumour goes.'

Claude found it hard to swallow his saliva. He knew a witch but was not fully aware of their capabilities. He looked toward the ramshackle house. The front lantern lights were now out.

'I think they have finally passed out,' Claude said.

Valiant strode toward the window and peered out.

'I think you are right, boy. In a few minutes they will be in a deep, drunken slumber. Get your shoes on, it is time.'

Claude already had his shoes on. He waited for Valiant by the door, but when he was ready, he motioned him through the house. Claude followed reluctantly, wondering why they were going in the opposite direction.

'Clearly, you lack the need for stealth, Claude Wells of Yorktown. There is a chance there is a watch over the house, as I would assume they would expect someone to come looking for your master.'

Valiant went into an empty room where several rats were gnawing at an old rug. Claude kept far from them.

'I didn't think of that,' he said, sheepishly.

'Clearly,' Valiant said, swinging one leg out of a paneless window, 'you have never been a pirate before.'

Claude followed him out into an overgrown allotment. They shimmied beside the house, moving quickly and keeping their backs against the aged timber. Valiant looked left and right but could only see an old vagabond camping out on a balcony a house over. The old man was asleep.

'Ah,' Valiant said. 'I believe my assumptions are true. We must continue on this way and keep our heads low!'

The pirate backtracked and then led the way along

the rear of several houses until they reached an intersection in the road. Without prewarning, Valiant jolted across the road, quick as lightning. Taken aback, Claude was left on his own in the dark. He lost track of where the pirate had gone. Then, from a slither of darkness, he could hear him hissing. A hand emerged from the darkness and waved him over. Claude ran through the puddles of mud and horse manure and joined him beside an old saloon. Dark clouds started to cover the moon.

'We go to the side door,' Valiant whispered. 'I doubt there will be a guard there, and if there is, he is more than likely passed out.'

Valiant, without warning again, took off running into the night. This time, Claude didn't wait to see where he was going, instead, he followed tightly at his heels. They ran through an old, hollowed building where Claude could see the remnants of old fires and fishbones. Valiant jolted through a window frame and knelt down beside the house. As Claude was climbing through, Valiant grabbed him and pulled him into the mud. Several paces ahead of them was the house. They were staring at the side door that Valiant had alluded to. No guard was in attendance.

'I will need you to hold a flame to the lock, so I can pick it,' Valiant said, handing Claude some matches.

Claude struck the match against the red phosphorus. It lit the darkened alley quickly, before disappearing. The salty air from the sea travelled through the streets and made it go out. Valiant looked at Claude with perplexed confusion. Claude struck it again and used his body to block the wind. Valiant turned to the rusted lock. His hands moved quickly as he placed long bent pins in the keyhole. He jingled the lock-pick and held one between his teeth. From down the alleyway came the stomping footfalls of someone coming their way.

'Someone's coming!' Claude said, as loud as he could whisper.

'I think I've got it,' Valiant stammered. The door clicked loudly and swung open.

Valiant and Claude fell through, toppling over each other. Claude gathered his foot and swung back to the door, closing it. The heavy boots trudged through the mud up to the door. Claude could see the shadow in the gap between the door and the floor. The doorknob turned, then jingled. Upon shutting it, it had relocked. The boots continued on their way.

'Must have been a patrol,' Valiant said, tucking his tools away.

Claude let his eyes adjust to the darkness. They appeared to be in some sort of storage room. There was a clear path leading through the boxes and empty crates to another door. To the left was a window. It was covered in salt and dirt, and it was barely see-through.

'This way,' Valiant said, keeping crouched down and heading toward the second door.

As they approached, Claude looked around at the boxes. He peeled the lid back of the nearest one and nearly gasped out loud. He stumbled backward, kicking the floor with fervour to get away. Valiant looked around confused. He then saw what Claude had been looking at. The box was full of human skulls.

'What... what, why?' Claude could only say.

Valiant looked crestfallen. He ran to the next box and opened it up. Inside were robes and wands and books haphazardly tossed in.

'Damn it,' he said. The words tumbled from his mouth with dejection.

'What is it? Who are those people?'

Valiant closed the box lid. 'It looks like mages from the mainland.'

'Magicians? Why are they all...' suddenly Claude realised.

'They must have been using them to try and decipher the book.'

'And if they can't do it... they kill them.'

Suddenly there was a loud bang at the door. Claude looked toward Valiant.

'Hide,' he yelped.

The door swung open, and a very drunk pirate walked in. He had put his shirt on inside out and back to front. He was still holding onto a nearly finished bottle of rum. His eyes went cross-eyed for a moment and then returned. Around his waist was a leather belt, upon a small hook jangled a ring of keys. Claude had managed to roll under a small broken bed frame that had been used to keep boxes off the floor. In the opposite corner he could see half of Valiant's face. He was trying to push his body behind what appears to be a large coffin. The drunken man fell forward and caught himself on some boxes, toppling them over. Claude's view of Valiant was now blocked.

'Bugger,' the man said, hiccupping. He started searching through boxes and tossing the contents out onto the floor. A wand rolled across the ground and came to a halt within the shadow of the bed frame. Claude looked at it. It was a beautiful black wand with a lilac tip that had been dipped in wax. The handle was animal hide. It looked like a relic. As he reached for it, the pirate stumbled back again and fell onto the bed. Boxes were knocked to the floor and scattered all around him. Claude was now looking up at his back. The pirate appeared to like his new situation. He let out an affirming moan now that he was lying down.

'I might just take a quick nap here.'

'William Buckets!' came a strong voice through the house.

The pirate shot up in an instant. He seemed to forget where he was. He leapt to his feet and snatched several books that had been resting on a mantle. He took off running, slamming the door behind him. Claude nabbed the wand and buried it in his cloak. After a few moments of waiting, Claude climbed out of his hiding place. He dusted off the dirt and spiderwebs and looked toward where Valiant had been hiding. He was not there.

'Claude,' Valiant said, coming from his right.

'How did you get over there?'

Valiant held up the ring of keys. 'Claude Wells of Yorktown, if I was not good at hiding, I would not make a very good pirate, now, would I? Now, let's go.'

They listened at the door, making sure there was no sound of footfalls, or talking. Valiant opened it an inch and the house was quiet.

'It's all clear, Claude.'

Valiant stepped out into the hallway and paused. A pistol drew from the shadows to his right and the barrel was held against his temple.

'Oh dear,' said a gruff voice. 'What have we here?'

CHAPTER 14
DOOMED TO FAIL

Colm Meagher grinned an audacious grin. Valiant stood with his hands in the air. Claude was still out of view, so stayed behind the rotten, wooden door.

'The Golden Serpent captain in the flesh,' Colm said, pointing with his gun toward the end of the hallway. 'We thought you had died when we tossed you overboard. I guess snakes can swim.'

Claude was taken aback by this statement. He now thought he may have been walked into a trap.

'Colm,' Valiant said, a large smile strewn across his weather-beaten face. 'It's been so long! How's the crew?' The pistol was pushed back into his temple. 'Very well. You weren't really much for small talk. I've come to get what is rightfully mine.'

'And what would that be?' Colm replied.

Claude reached into his cloak and pulled out his wand. He could see Colm's rat-like face through the door slit.

'I believe Mathian still has my boots. The ones made of snakeskin with the golden skull on the boot tip.'

'Mathian is dead,' Colm replied, matter-of-factly.

'Oh, well I guess he will take them to the grave then.'

Claude leapt from the doorway. His hand raised

with the wand pointing at Colm's head. As the pirate's eyes turned to look at the boy, Claude opened his mouth instinctively. A garble of backward words spilled from his tongue, casting a flash of yellow light from the tip of the wand. It hit Colm straight between the eyes. Instantly, his eyes shut, and he slumped to the floor like a sack of potatoes. Valiant looked at the crumpled body of Colm at his feet and lent down to check his pulse.

'He's still alive. It looks like he's sleeping,' he grabbed the pistol and looked up at Claude. 'How did you do that? Are you a magician?'

Claude tucked the wand away. 'I don't know how I do it. It just happens. I was compelled to face him, and what happened after that seemed natural... like it was out of my control.'

Valiant kept the pistol in his hands. 'Ether way, we should get him in that storage room and lock it.'

They dragged him into the room they had just exited and tied his hands up with rope that Claude had found in one of the boxes. They lay him gently down on his side and locked the door behind him.

'Where to?' Claude said, feeling a little shocked after his sudden use of magic.

'He's got to be in the basement, so we have to find the entry.'

They gingerly tip-toed through the hallway and into the next room. There was a round table with playing cards strewn across it. Two men sat at the table fast asleep. Several bottles of ale sat around the floor, empty. Valiant looked like a marionette as he quietly moved between the bottles. Claude could feel his heart beating in his neck. Valiant pointed to a ring of keys dangling from one of the pirates' belts. Valiant indicating with his fingers for Claude to watch the door.

Claude leaned back and looked out into the corridor. It was clear. He gave Valiant the thumbs up. The man who had the keys on a belt loop was snoring loudly. His face was covered in ingrown beard hairs and every time he breathed in, he would let out a loud snore that would shake the bottles.

Valiant stepped behind the snoring man and reached down to the keys. There were at least ten keys on the ring that Claude could see. All different shapes, sizes, and rust progression. Valiant's slender fingers gently pinched the key ring as the man leapt up from his seat, slamming down the cards he had in his hands and confirmed he had won the game.

Claude shot to the ground, trying to make himself blend in with the general mess of the room. The man looked at his friend and then fell back down onto the chair and resumed sleeping. After a few seconds, when his heart had stopped trying to bounce out of his chest, Claude looked over the table. Valiant was gone, so were the ring of keys.

'Claude Wells,' said the familiar voice to his right. Valiant was crouched below an old broken chest. He held the keys up so Claude could see them and gave him a thumbs up.

Claude had no idea how the pirate was moving so quickly. They went through the room and unlocked the next door. The room was smaller, with no light except that from the moon coming in through the window. Several of the boards had fallen off, allowing enough moonlight to shine directly on a locked trap door. Claude shut the door behind him. He stood beside the trap door and looked down at it. His wand in its holster came a small vibration.

'I think he's down there,' Claude said.

'I think you're right, Claude Wells. If he's not down there, then he must be upstairs, but that would be too dangerous. People could hear him calling for help,' he knelt down and tried several keys before finding the correct one. With a click, the latch unlocked. Valiant pulled the trap door open. A darken staircase went down into awful blackness.

Suddenly, the door behind them started to rattle.

'They're coming!' Valiant screamed, unnecessarily. 'Get down their Claude Wells, I'll hold them off as long as I can!' He grabbed Claude by the scruff of his shirt sleeve and yanked him toward the hole.

Claude rushed down the stairs, only to hear the trap door slam shut behind him and the key snap off in the lock. Following, came the sound of fighting. Something rammed hard against the door and then everything went silent.

Claude wasn't sure if Valiant had trapped him deliberately or not. He looked down toward the bottom of the staircase and decided to proceed down.

The stairs were covered in dust with cobwebs creepily hanging overhead. He reached the concrete floor and was taken aback from what he saw. Abraham was on his knees, hunched forward with his hands resting on the floor in front of him. His shirt had been burnt off and he was covered in sores. His whole body had been cut and whipped. Trickles of blood had dried. Around his wrists, where he was chained to the floor, his skin had started to turn purple.

'Abraham?' Claude said, sheepishly, making sure no one was down there with them.

Abraham lifted his head up. His nose was broken and all around his lips was dried blood.

'Claude?' he said, meekly.

Claude rushed over to him and slid down on his knees, yanking at the chains.

'It's not good, lad. They're bolted to the ground. How did you find me?'

Claude patted his pockets for the ring of keys, but he suddenly remembered that Valiant had them.

'I had help.'

Abraham pushed off the floor and straightened his back. His beard was matted with blood that had dripped off his nose and lips.

'Were they trying to get you to decipher a book?' Claude said, examining the screws that held the plate onto the concrete.

'They tried, but ... as soon as I saw it... I knew what they had found, and I want no part of it.'

'They want to release someone called Pablo

Marquis?'

Abraham lifted his puffy, swollen eyes and looked at his apprentice. He managed to smile.

'You've done well, Claude. You've found out much information… and you found me before it is too late.'

Echoing down the staircase, came the sound of a sledgehammer hitting the lock.

'They're trying to get down here, you should hide, Claude. If they catch you…'

There was only a partial cupboard in the corner. It had two concrete sides and little else. Claude ran to it and took the black wand from his cloak, tossing the hood over his head and kneeling down in the shadows. Thunderous footsteps stampeded down to where Abraham was sitting. It was Colm Meagher and another pirate.

'Well, he's still here!' said the second pirate.

Colm turned and slapped him across the face. 'Shut your hole, Firin.'

Firin felt his cheek with his hand. It was hot.

'Someone's come into our headquarters, Wandmaker. And we assume they are trying to free you.'

Abraham looked up at the demented man. 'I wouldn't know, I've been trapped down here for days.'

'Yes,' Colm grinned. 'I know. It smells like it.'

Firin began to laugh, until Colm gave him a firm stare. Colm wiped blood from Abraham's face. He leant so close that Abraham could see his own reflection in his eyes.

'As soon as you translate the book... you can be on your way. You don't have to die in a basement, Wandmaker.'

Something came over Claude. Instinct and heart took control of his legs and he sprung from his position, pointing the unknown wand toward the pair.

'Stop it,' Claude said, unsure of what he was going to say next. It was the only words that came out.

Colm and Firin looked startled. Colm quickly regained his composure.

'Young lad, how did you get down here? I suppose it does not matter, as you're attempt to have us release your master is doomed to fail. Your wand,' Colm said trying to study it in the dark, 'is that of a dead wizard named Ofaris Gothar. He was aloof and hard as nails. He put up a good fight... pity his wand never worked.'

Claude took a step forward, his wand still raised and pointed at the pair.

'I've got it to work, now unlock those chains.'

Firin looked to his master. Colm's eyes were staring at Claude.

'I don't think you understand me, lad.'

Claude took another half step forward and his mouth opened, reciting an ancient incantation that made the wand emit a cobalt blue beam of energy wavering across the room like lightning. It hit the smirking Firin, sending him through the air doing cartwheels until he hit the wall and slumped to the ground. Colm had watched the pirate launch through the air and then looked back at Claude.

'How?'

'Don't worry about how,' Claude said, his hand now shaking. 'Just unlock the chains.'

Colm pulled out a ring of keys from his belt and stepped toward the Wandmaker.

'How well do you know your master, lad?'

Claude looked over to Firin who was still moaning and moving around in pain. He turned his attention back to Colm.

'Don't talk, just unlock the chains.'

Colm bent down, but only held the keys near the lock.

'Do you know what he *really* is?'

Abraham lifted his tired and sore head. 'Shut up, Colm. Do as the lad says.'

He inserted the key and the wrist strap snapped open. Abraham pulled his hand away quickly.

'Do you know, Claude Wells, that Abraham Crenshaw is not who he appears to be? I bet he's told you somethings about the underground world of magic, but not his true identity.'

Colm had gotten into Claude's head. He was now looking toward Abraham for his reaction.

'You speak again, and you'll end up like your friend over there,' Claude said, pressing the end of the wand to Colm's head.

Colm grinned his teethy, crooked grin. 'He's a

cursed man, Claude! Long ago was he cursed. Perhaps you have seen him in his other form? A bear!'

Claude's eyes peeled open as the wand dispersed another surge of energy. This time, the streaming whip of matter was bright red. It sent Colm across the room, as if hit by a thousand Clydesdale horses. He was unconscious before he hit the wall. Claude quickly tucked his wand away and retrieved the keys. He could not think of what Colm had just said at the moment. Truth or not, they needed to get out of there. He unlocked the remaining locks and helped Abraham to his feet.

'Lad…' Abraham said, his eyes fading slowly. 'I was… going to… tell you.'

'Not now,' Claude said. 'We have to get out of here.'

Suddenly the door to the basement flew open, sending a long shaft of candlelight across the staircase. At the very bottom, Claude and Abraham looked up. It was Agnes and Valiant.

CHAPTER 15
MANY MOONS AGO

'Well done, Claude Wells of Yorktown,' Valiant screamed in delight. Agnes hushed him and pushed him down the stairs to help Claude bring Abraham up.

'We don't have long,' Agnes said. 'I've caused a distraction.'

Claude could smell fire.

'She set my house of fire,' Valiant said, forcing a smile. 'It's about to jump to this place.'

'Agnes,' Abraham said as he reached the top of the staircase. 'The book…'

Agnes reached into her kaftan and slowly pulled out a book. The cover was darkened, black leather. Several red ribbons streamed out the end, bookmarked at various areas. In gold leaf script were the words *Frenguard – The Tome of Many Whispers*.

'I have it,' Agnes said, placing her hand on his shoulder to reassure him.

She tucked it back into her blouse and headed for the door. It had already been kicked open. Through the hallway was the main entrance. There were bodies of pirates all strewn across the floor, some looked to have been beaten, while others had no apparent injury, but were deeply unconscious. Valiant had Abraham's arm over his shoulder. Abraham was looking up at him though bruised eyes.

'He's here to help us,' Claude said, seeing curiosity across Abraham's face. 'He's a pirate, but he has a boat waiting to take us to Shrub Oak.'

'I would say I am more of an entrepreneur dealing in risky items, who knows *how* to sail a boat.'

Claude whipped his head around to him.

'You said you had a boat? The Golden Serpent!'

Agnes flung the front door open, and they stumbled out onto the muddy roadway. The house opposite them was roaring with fire. No one was putting it out or paying much attention to it.

Claude felt a heavy burden in his chest. His heart was sore, and he could not ignore it.

'Abraham,' he said, 'please tell me...'

They had soon noticed Agnes had paused in front of them. Soft rain started to fall. Abrahams busted eye sockets lifted up, staring to the end of the road. Claude looked to where he was staring. At the very end of the muddy causeway, hidden in silhouette, was a figure. It stood with his legs slightly apart and its hands behind its back. It wore a wide brimmed hat with the cap several inches bigger than any he had ever seen.

Agnes stepped in front of the trio and stared the man down.

'I will assume you are Morse Wolcott. The orchestrator of these men and the mages sent to Shrub Oak.'

Morse cocked his head back and laughed. 'My dear witch, you have it in one.' He took a slow stride toward them, his heavy leather boots sinking slightly in the mud. 'My right-hand man, Colm, has told me about the tidings happening in your city and I decided to finally come and see it with my own eyes.'

'I will burn the book before I ever translate it!' Abraham roared.

Morse took one last step and then froze. 'Wandmaker Crenshaw. As I understand it, you have not been overly truthful to your apprentice.'

'Don't listen to him, Claude. He will only tell lies,' Abraham said, shrugging off Valiant's assistance.

Morse turned his head toward Claude. 'I see you've found the black wand,' he said, his words dripping with conviction. 'Black is the wand and purple being the tip, a cursed combination. If you don't already feel its sickly curse coursing through your body, you soon will.'

Claude didn't answer. He gripped the wand, ignoring everything the wizard had said.

'Move, so we shall pass,' Claude said. Agnes readied herself, filling her hands with herbs and powder from her side satchel.

'Your master used to work for me, young apprentice. Many moons ago. He wasn't much older than yourself.'

'Shut up, Morse!' Abraham snapped, stumbling forward.

'We were on the hunt for the Broughton Witches, when your master here decided to be a hero and enter their domain alone. The witches weren't so kind to you, were they Abraham Crenshaw.'

Abraham tried to rush forward, but his knees gave way and he fell forward into the mud. The rain started to strike down on him, making the dry blood runny again.

'Lies,' Abraham mumbled.

'His legacy will not be that of a Wandmaker... no,' Morse said, stepping up closer to Abraham. 'It will be that of a shape shifter. Specifically, a bear,' Morse looked toward Claude. 'A bear and an out-of-control murderer. Who do you think killed your brother?'

'Enough!' Abraham lunged forward, just as Morse brought his wand up and released a devastating spell. It peeled through existence like a balloon expanding. Claude felt the black wand tear out of his grip and fly over his head. All the spell ingredients in Agnes's hand incinerated, leaving her flesh scorched. Abraham toppled backward, his feet and arms becoming longer and fleshier. Long shaggy hair grew from his body and his nose started grow in the shape of a bear snout. His nails ripped from flesh as claws grew out of his fingers and dug into the rich mud. Abraham had entirely turned into a bear.

Abraham leapt toward Morse, slashing him across the chest and knocking him down.

'Get to the boat!' he screamed. His voice was no longer of Abraham, instead it came out guttural and animalistic.

Valiant ran between Agnes and Claude, who soon followed. Behind them they could hear the fight continue; slapping skin into mud and the roaring of the fires. Valiant led the way and ran down the staggered path to the make-shift port. It was lined with massive sea-faring ships. Valiant stopped suddenly and took his hat off and scratched his head.

'Please don't tell me you lost your ship?' Claude said annoyed.

'Do not fret, Claude Wells, I am simply deciding which ship will be the new Golden Serpent.'

He ran to the very end of the pier and down the rickety, unstable wooden plank. Agnes moved quickly, surprising Claude as he had never seen her move any faster than a slow stride.

'When you say, new Golden Serpent?' Claude said, following close behind Valiant's heels.

Valiant reached the very last sailboat and started to untie the rope.

'No time to discuss this, Claude Wells, help me untie the ropes!'

Claude did what he was told. He was trying to keep the last few minutes out of his mind. If he let it in, it would eat up his entire consciousness. *Abraham turned into a bear in front of my very own eyes! Why hadn't he told me this? Did he really kill my brother?*

'Claude!' Agnes shouted at him. Claude snapped out of his daydream. He felt the witch's cold hand on his shoulder.

'Now is not the time to overthink things... we will get you answers soon. But first, we must get off this island.'

Claude agreed and swung the rope around the bollards. Agnes leapt onto the ship and started untying the ropes from the cleats, rounding them up and placing them to the side. Valiant had turned the wheel to the right and raised the sails. The ship was staring to move. Claude took several steps back and ran at the ship, leaping into the air and landing with a roll on the ships deck. It hurt his back and leg, but there was no time to waste. He got to his feet, but his ankle was starting to swell. A gust of wind ripped through the island, catching in the sails, and sending it rocketing away from the pier.

'This way!' Agnes yelped, pointing up to the mountain top.

Two bears now were fighting each other in a bloody battle. Claude could see them both, thrashing their claws. Fur was flying like dropping snow. Morse was now also a bear!

'Abraham!' Claude screamed. He could feel his heart sink down into his stomach. 'Jump!' He turned to Valiant who was at the wheel. 'Get us as close as you can!'

Agnes rushed to the steering column and helped Valiant turn it and hold it as the rushing water splashed up onto the decking. The bears roared with anger, slashing each other, and drawing blood. They were a mangle of teeth and deathly yellow eyes.

'Lad!' Valiant screamed over the crashing waves. 'We'll only have a few seconds before we crash into the side of the rock wall. You are going to have to get him to jump!'

Claude looked up as the bears rolled closer and closer to the ledge. He could hear them roaring and gnawing at each other.

'Abraham! Jump!' Claude screamed, trying to reach him over the sound of the crashing of the ocean against the ship.

One of the bears suddenly stood up and looked down toward the boat. Several sails were puffed outward, holding the wind, and coursing the ship dangerously close to the side of the island. Agnes looked up with her steely eyes. The ship lurched sideways, crushing against the stone and shredding pieces of wood off the starboard. Claude heard the crunching and grew increasingly terrified.

Suddenly, the bears separated and one of the bears ran along the fifty-foot-high side, on all fours. It leapt over rocks and fallen parts of the shanty buildings. The fire had grown enormous as the bear ran through the fiery debris. It then leapt into the air as the ship was pulled away from the side before it tore a hole in it. The bear flew through the air, landing on the sail. It used it claws to slide down the wind-beaten fabric to break its fall. It hit the deck hard, cracking some of the wood. The body of the bear started to morph back into Abraham.

'Abraham!' Claude rushed to him.

From above, the second bear leapt to join them on the deck, but Valiant, with the help of Agnes, yanked the boat away and the animal fell into the rough sea.

Claude looked back to see the bear scratching at the sides of the rocky wall, trying to purchase grip. Stones and loose dirt fell onto it and eventually it surrendered to the sea.

CHAPTER 16
SECRETS

Abraham opened his eyes and could smell fire. He looked to his left and saw his fireplace gently warming the room. Large, fresh logs towered in the pit while a pot hung over the flames, its contents smelling divine. He tried to move, but all his muscles hurt. His knees felt swollen and bruised. He looked at his fingers and someone had cleaned the blood around his nails and wrapped them in gauze. He touched his nose and winced. It was surely broken but was covered in a bandage. He was in his home but couldn't remember how he got there.

'Claude?' he said. His voice came out raspy and he coughed frantically.

There was movement from the larder and Agnes appeared holding a tray.

'You're awake,' she said, placing the tray down beside him. On the tray was hot tea and several pieces of bread filled with nuts and herbs. 'You should eat up, Abraham. You've been out for a while.'

'Where's Claude?' he asked again.

'He's upstairs, in his room.'

Abraham looked at the witch. His eyes were glassy. He then turned back to the fire.

'What happened? The last thing I remember was seeing Morse Wolcott and being surrounded by fire.'

Agnes dipped her head and took a seat on a stool close to Abraham.

'You turned.'

Abraham nodded. 'I knew I had. It must have been in the presence of another changer.'

'Morse turned also. You were trying to kill each other. You held him off while we escaped to a boat.'

'A boat?' Abraham said, surprised.

'Claude had found a captain of a ship. We managed to get close enough for you to leap to safety. But when you hit the deck, you landed on your head. We got back to the Shrub Oak port and got the local fisherman to drag you back here on their fishing cart.'

'When was that?'

'Two and a half days ago.'

Abraham let a tear drop from his eye and quickly wiped it away.

'Claude knows?' he asked.

'Yes. Morse told him you killed his brother.'

Abraham's head dropped. 'Have you spoken to him?'

'He packed his belongings to go home, but I told him to at least wait until you woke, so you can explain.'

The black cat, Maspeth, strolled in and rubbed its face on Abraham's leg. She purred loudly. Resting by the fire was the white cat, Akron. She had opened her eyes and looked at Abraham and reclosed them.

'Can you get him for me?' Abraham asked Agnes.

Agnes steadied herself and went to the stairs. She

glanced back at Abraham. He was sipping his tea and looking worried. She took the stairs one at a time and held onto the wall. She walked along the hallway and could hear Claude crying. She knocked on the door and it swung open several inches. Claude was sitting on his bed with the ginger cat Oka lying next to him.

'He is awake, Claude.'

Claude looked up at the old witch. She looked at his bags packed and sitting by the door.

'What do I do, Agnes?'

'Come down and talk to him. Then make up your mind.'

Claude agreed. He stood up much to the annoyance of Oka for being disturbed. He went downstairs and noticed Agnes hadn't followed him. Claude stood at the bottom of the staircase and looked to Abraham. He wasn't looking at him. Instead, he was staring at the fire.

'Sit down, lad. I have much to explain.'

Claude did as he was instructed and sat at the couch opposite him. The room was warm, and he could smell the tea and fresh bread.

'You've been asleep for days,' Claude said, unsure what to say. 'How are you feeling?'

'Claude, you're a good kid,' Abraham said, turning to him. His twin black eyes made his eye sockets look skeletal. 'I want you to know that I didn't tell you about my condition, as I didn't want to scare you.'

'I've seen you as a bear before, haven't I? When I was cutting wood and attacked by another bear.'

'Yes,' Abraham said without hesitation. 'I was coming back to fetch you, when I could smell another changer in the vicinity.'

'Was it Morse Wolcott?'

'I believe so,' Abraham answered.

'He is dead now,' Claude said.

Abraham didn't want to approach the topic in this way, but it had already started.

'I didn't kill your brother, Claude.'

Claude broke down in tears. 'Was it Morse?' he said through sobs.

'It could have been. I don't often remember much when I transform, but I have images of that night.'

Claude waited for him to tell the story, before speaking.

'Your brother was running errands for a gravedigger when he was attacked. I heard there was another changer in Yorktown, so I went there to investigate. I had been there for three days before I started to track him.'

Shadows danced across Claudes face. 'Why would a changer be in Yorktown?'

'I don't know, Claude. After he attacked your brother I ran after him, but he changed back to human form and slipped into the back streets that were full of people. I tried to find him again, but his scent was gone.'

Claude didn't reply straight away. He was hoping this new information would lift a huge weight off his shoulders, but it made it even more heavy. Agnes was suddenly at the bottom of the staircase. She held Oka like a baby in her arms, patting her.

'I didn't kill your brother, Claude. I can promise you that.'

Claude wiped tears away.

'Can you control it?' he asked, meekly.

'With the help from Agnes,' Abraham said, turning his attention to the witch. 'I can keep it at bay.'

'A mixture of herbs and powder found in specific flowers growing out of fresh water keeps the curse quiet.'

'It's a curse?'

'Morse had mentioned it, before he changed,' Agnes said, checking the pot over the stove.

'I don't have much recollection anymore of the witches who did this to me but I've been fighting with it most of my life.'

Claude suddenly felt the stress and pressure that had been pushing him down start to alleviate.

'The life of a Wandmaker isn't an easy life, Claude,' Agnes said, poking the fire with a poker. 'It can be rewarding, and detrimental.'

'I should have told you earlier, Claude. But I could never find the right time.'

Agnes turned to Abraham. The end of her poker was red hot. 'Tell him everything, Abraham. I won't allow any more secrets.'

Claude looked confused. 'There's more?' Inside he felt deceived. He wanted to grab his bags and run home to Yorktown.

Abraham steadied his feet on the ground and took some time to stand. His body was hunched forward, and he wobbled.

'For the last few years, I have been hiding witches in the house,' Abraham said, avoiding eye contact with Claude.

'Witches?' Claude repeated, looking around the room.

'They were being hunted by a powerful black magician, so I offered them refuge.'

Agnes raised her hand and started mouthing an incantation. The pot over the stove bubbled and hissed. The three cats suddenly all gathered in front of the fire and began to shriek and shake uncontrollably. Claude bolted to his feet and backed away. The felines began to thrash their legs. They rolled around on the ground and began to morph into a fleshy creation of hair and long ears. Their tails sunk into their body, and they started to stand up on their hind legs. Their fur receded and their noses grew. Finally, they stood up and shook out the remaining transformation. Before him, stood three women. They looked at Claude with huge grins.

'It's nice to meet you finally, Claude,' said Maspeth, who was the tallest of the trio.

'Claude!' yelped Akron, her long blonde hair hanging low over her shoulders. 'I'm so sorry you didn't know.'

Oka had long ginger hair, flecked with silver strands. She went to Agnes, and they hugged.

'Thank you, Agnes. I was getting tired of being a cat.'

Claude stumbled backward. He was completely lost for words.

'Claude, these are the witches hiding in my house. From time-to-time Agnes here has changed them to their human form, to let them stretch their legs, but it's always been while we were at the store or elsewhere. There are no more secrets.'

Claude could hardly believe his eyes. He was in a state of surreal shock. He looked to Abraham who had a smile on his face.

That night Maspeth and Akron brought in a large plank of wood and made a huge table in the lounge room. Valiant, who had been sleeping in the small gardening shed on the property came in for supper and was more than happy to have a hot meal. Akron kept giggling at him when he slurped his stew. Valiant had turned red with embarrassment.

Claude had slowly come to accept the secrets that had been revealed. Abraham promised to tell him everything from now on. Over the proceeding hour he had stopped apologising and concentrated on healing.

'What about the book?' Claude said, while Oka took his empty bowl and brought it to the kitchen.

Agnes nodded, '*Frenguard, the Tome of Many Whispers*, needs to be taken to the Wandmakers Council in Rome. They need to translate it and lock it away from people like Morse Wolcott.'

'We will take it,' Abraham said, abruptly.

'We're going to Rome?' Claude responded,

flabbergasted.

Valiant leant against the wall and grinned. 'Well, we do have a boat.'

Both Abraham and Claude turned toward the pirate. Abraham still wasn't entirely sure of the pirate, but he had done some heavy lifting of firewood and fetched supplies while Abraham had been ill. Trust was slowly beginning to build.

'We will leave for Rome when I am able to deal with travelling by sea. Agnes will keep the book secure for now,' Abraham said.

They all gathered around the fire and drunk tea, retelling the story until they grew tired and slept.

CHAPTER 17
VISIT ME

Several days had passed when Abraham started to feel himself again. He was able to walk unassisted and his appetite returned. Valiant was granted temporary residence in the house, which he relished, as he enjoyed the company of the three witches.

Agnes had returned home after she nursed Abraham back to health. Claude had decided to leave for his parent's house in a few days' time. Abraham had insisted he visit his family. If the journey to Rome was going to take several weeks, then he should see them before he left on his long voyage.

The book had been taken by Agnes for safe keeping. She had many hiding spots in the woodland, where spells could be used to hide its location. Claude much preferred it to be out of the house anyway. It had a strange aura round it whenever he was near it.

The witches and Valiant agreed to stay home while Abraham and Claude went to open the shop. Although he wasn't up for lathing wood, or making intricate wands, the store still needed to operate. The walk to Shrub Oak village centre took longer than usual, as they had to stop for Abraham to rest and catch his breath.

'Maybe we should turn back?' Claude said, wearing his green cape and hood over his head.

The trees provided shade, but the wind was cold and harsh.

'Nonsense. I am fine,' Abraham debated, waving his young apprentice away.

They continued on their way and reached the front gate by mid-morning. Claude had nearly forgotten how busy the market bazaar could get. People everywhere bartered for goods and services. Horses clopped along the rickety cobblestone roads. The air was filled with the smell of cooking meat and freshly frying eggs. They walked through the horde of people, seemingly unnoticed. As they reached the street the store was on, Abraham started to slow his pace.

'What is it?' Claude asked.

Abraham had come to a full stop. His hand went to his mouth. Claude thought he was about to be sick, until he saw what Abraham was looking at. Crenshaw Carpentry and Woodwork store had been burnt to the ground. Black smoke still smouldered from the wreckage. Stone around the building was burnt and scorched black. Claude ran up to the structure and looked in. It was completely gutted. Every piece of furniture had been turned to ash.

'Mr Crenshaw!' came the voice of Lou the candlemaker from further down the street. He wore a purple neckerchief. He waved his hands enthusiastically. 'Mr Crenshaw! We tried to locate you, but no one could find you.'

Abraham turned away from the store. Anger rose up in his chest. He knew it had been the work of Colm and the Harrowers.

'I sent my youngest lad to your house, but there was no one home. We didn't know what to do,' his face was crestfallen. He felt horrible for Abraham.

'We have been away,' Claude said, meekly, to the candlemaker.

'How did it happen?' Abraham asked, his eyes shut and remained closed.

'Three nights ago, we heard the bell of the fire brigade. I looked out the window and saw the flames licking the air. We used buckets and anything else we could find to try put it out. But it was too late. I'm so sorry Abraham.'

'Thank you, Lou. I appreciate you trying.'

The candlemaker slowly stepped away, leaving Abraham and Claude to investigate the damage.

Claude stepped in gingerly and tested the structure of the floor. Abraham stepped up behind him and made his way into the showroom. All his beautiful, hand-crafted furniture was destroyed. Most of it had been burnt so badly it was now a pile of ash and tinder.

'The Harrowers?' Claude said, knowing the answer all too well.

Abraham nodded. He went through the shop to the back of the store and saw the table had been pushed over and the secret entrance to his wandmaking workshop revealed. He leant down and looked around the brickwork. Claude stood opposite him, looking distraught.

'They fire-bombed the wands. Then,' Abraham pointed, 'it spread from there. Its punishment for not translating the book.'

Claude saw a darkened area leading from the wand pit, out into the showroom. His heart sunk, but he managed to keep the tears from falling. Together they walked through the store and tried to salvage anything they could, but it was all gone. Claude felt lost and bereaved. It had only just started to sculpt the wands on his own.

They walked outside and stood in the bright sunlight. City folk moved around and paid them little notice.

'I have much to work out here, Claude. The place was insured, but not for much. There will be paperwork to fill out and a long investigation. I would suggest you leave for your parent's house early and stay for a week. Once you return, I will have sorted everything out and we can organise our trip to Rome.'

Claude felt his head dip. 'I want to stay with you and help clean up. I can help you with anything you need.'

Abraham put his hand on Claude's shoulder. Several of his fingers were wrapped in bandages still. They said their farewells and Claude began to run through the streets of Shrub Oak. He dashed across streets and through market stalls. He leapt over fences and cut through the pig farmer's herd. When he was out on the road, he ran faster. His heart felt lifted from the pit of his stomach.

Every now and then he would stop to catch his breath. The sun was beaming down, hot, yet the air was cold. Winter wasn't too far off now, and he could feel it in the mornings. As he crested the hill leading to Yorktown, he could see bellowing smoke from the smokestacks of the timber mill. The city looked like it had grown.

He ran down the embankment and tried to steady his pace to a slow walk as he went through the gates. It was much busier than Shrub Oak. Every street he turned down, he was bumped into by hurrying city folk. He desperately wanted to run to the cemetery to see his brother and tell him about all the adventures he had been on. But he knew he should go home first. There would be time for that later.

He weaved his way through the dilapidated neighbourhood where he once lived. Garbage had started to pile up in excess. All the buildings looked further run down then he remembered. There was no traffic down in this area, from horses nor buggies, like there used to be. Half the buildings looked abandoned and either half torn down or boarded up. He felt a lump in his throat as he turned down the street toward his parents' house.

The front door was open. Claude ran to it, suddenly very worried. He pushed the door opened and the inside was completely empty.

He felt numb and unable to fathom what was going on. His old bed below the window was gone. The furniture was gone. The empty icebox was gone. The stove remained but were covered in cobwebs. He moved through the house, feeling like a ghost, until he reached his parents' bedroom.

On the floor was a sealed envelope. He gingerly walked over to it. His eyes began to flood with tears. It had his name scrawled across it in his mother's handwriting. He opened it.

Dear Claude,

I am so sorry we didn't write to you sooner. Your father has taken a turn for the worse and has been admitted to Yorktown Hospital.

I have been at his side for the last week, keeping constant vigil. I wanted to tell you, but I knew you would come immediately, and I didn't want to take you away from your work.

I have returned home to pack the few belongings we have and have found that we have been evicted for not paying the rent. They sold most of our household items to recoup their funds, but I managed to get some clothes.

You can find me at the mission complex on Edger Road, beside the hospital. I'm staying in a one-bedroom, shared bathroom, house for women. Visiting hours are from 11am to 2pm. Every day I sit by your father's side and pray for him to get well. Unfortunately, the doctors say he only has a few days left.

When you return home and get this note, I hope you are not too mad and come to visit me.

Love,

Mum.

Claude let the letter drop from his hands. It hit the

dusty floor. He turned and went to the front door. He stepped out into the street and began to run.

THE END

BOOK III
THE WANDMAKERS AFFLICTION

*Abraham Crenshaw and his Wandmaker apprentice
Claude Wells have in their possession a very powerful,
dark magic book. They need to cross the great ocean to the
Wandmakers Society in Italy to have it bound and locked
away forever.*

*Agnes the witch knows the mission will be dangerous
as many factions are now looking for them. The long
journey is full of peril as they hide in the bowels of the
ship. After rough seas and long nights, they finally reach
their destination.*

*The society has become corrupted, and the headquarters
is overrun with night creatures.*

*Abraham must find out what has happened. He must
save the society from darkness and restore it to its glory,
all while keeping the book safe.*

ACKNOWLEDGEMENTS

Thanks to Sabrina and Ouroborus Books. Thanks to Jenny and Poe for having to hear about my story line ideas and putting up with me taking time out to write.

My family for buying my books and spreading the word. Everyone who comes out to see me and talks books, I appreciate every second.

For more information on Mitchell visit
www.ouroborusbooks.com

Milton Keynes UK
Ingram Content Group UK Ltd.
UKHW040038111123
432318UK00004B/69

9 780645 619249